ONE WEEK
WITH THE
FRENCH TYCOON

ONE WEEK WITH THE FRENCH TYCOON

BY

CHRISTY McKELLEN

MILLS
BOON®

First published in Great Britain 2016
By Mills & Boon, an imprint of HarperCollins*Publishers*
1 London Bridge Street, London, SE1 9GF

Large Print edition 2016

© 2016 Christy McKellen

ISBN: 978-0-263-26237-7

Our policy is to use papers that are natural, renewable
and recyclable products and made from wood grown
in sustainable forests. The logging and manufacturing
processes conform to the legal environmental regulations
of the country of origin.

Printed and bound in Great Britain
by CPI Antony Rowe, Chippenham, Wiltshire

This one's for my beautiful, witty and fiercely clever sisters-in-law, Kat and Buffy. Thank you for being the sisters I never had and welcoming me so warmly into your family. I love spending time with you. Here's to spending many more fabulous weekends in London together.

CHAPTER ONE

Arriving in Amalfi—a most lively and dramatic town in which to begin your journey...

WHEN INDIGO HUGHES had spent long hours daydreaming about her walking holiday along the Amalfi Coast of Southern Italy, *this* wasn't exactly what she'd envisioned.

Luggageless—after the airline had inexplicably sent her backpack containing her carefully organised walking gear to goodness knew where instead of Naples—and apparently dispossessed, because of a foul-up on the computer with her hotel booking, she was now facing the reality of spending the first night of her much anticipated holiday sleeping rough on the streets of Amalfi.

Whilst she wasn't averse to roughing it— she'd travelled to enough festivals and partaken in enough camping trips for that not to be an issue—she'd been looking forward to falling into a comfortable bed after a crazy week of late nights and early mornings, and was not in the mood to laugh this off.

'But my ex-boyfriend booked a room in this hotel months ago,' she explained again to the receptionist, her voice now projecting the disconcerting characteristic of a crow with a sore throat.

The intimidatingly poised receptionist pursed her blood-red lips and tightened her arms across her impressive cleavage. 'I'm sorry, *Signorina*. As I said, I have no record of your booking and we are fully booked. If you had the documents to prove it, or even the credit card it was booked with, I could perhaps do something for you, but as it is…' From the look on her face, she clearly wasn't keen on having someone as scruffy as Indigo messing up her beautifully appointed five-star hotel reception desk whilst also challenging her competency.

Panicky heat rushed to Indigo's face. 'As *I* explained, my *ex*-boyfriend booked the room so I don't have the credit card or documents. I assumed a booking reference number would be enough.'

The woman's helpless shrug, then her overemphasised shift in eye contact to the next person in line, tipped Indigo over the edge of frustration into fiery indignation. But before she could draw breath there was a movement behind her and a tall man in a beautifully cut casual suit stepped forwards to stand next to her at the desk.

'Pardon, mademoiselle,' he interjected smoothly, his fresh, spicy scent hitting her nose at the exact same moment his eyes locked with hers.

Indigo had never related to the expression of being 'swept off her feet' by a man before, but that was exactly how she felt right now. As if the power of his presence had physically lifted her into the air, her internal organs quivering as if she were in free fall. She gazed up at him, his unusual combination of whisky-brown eyes and sandy-blond hair keeping her transfixed as her pulse beat an enthusiastic rhythm in her throat. But apparently she didn't capture his interest in the same way because, after giving her a curt nod, he turned sharply away, bringing her back down to earth with a thump.

'I have a reservation,' he said to the receptionist in a deep, smoky, French-accented voice, which made Indigo think of the actors in the Gallic art house films she'd been so in love with during her college days.

Lounging against the desk, he held up his smartphone so the receptionist could see the screen and type the booking reference into her computer.

Indigo looked from one to the other in disbelief. She seemed to have been well and truly dismissed.

Something she'd become rather too familiar with recently.

Before she could open her mouth again to point out that they were both being utterly rude and that she wasn't going to be ignored like this, the receptionist shook her head and looked up at the Frenchman, her expression projecting a lot more contrition than when she'd dealt with Indigo.

'I'm sorry, *Signor*, I don't have a record of your booking.'

'That's not possible. Check again, please,' the man replied in a tone that clearly brooked no argument.

Indigo watched with a sense of self-righteous vindication as the receptionist typed the number in again, then checked something else on another screen, her shoulders stiffening as she finally accepted there was a problem with the booking system.

She seemed a little pale when she looked back up at him. 'My apologies, *Signor*,' she breathed. 'I don't know what could have happened. It appears there was a glitch with the computer and I've given your room away. I only have the honeymoon suite available now, but it would be my pleasure to let you stay there tonight. We will correct the mistake by tomorrow and I will have your original suite available for you then.'

Indigo frowned as she twigged what was going on.

'Hang on a second. Why didn't you offer *me* the honeymoon suite? I was here first!' she protested, feeling a cocktail of humiliation and umbrage warm her face again.

The woman's gaze slid to hers. 'Because the gentleman booked a *suite, Signorina*, so this room is more in his...*category*.' She gave Indigo a tight little smile as if to say, *That's not the word I was grasping for, but you get the message*.

'Okay—' the Frenchman began in his smooth, lyrical accent.

But even the strength of his charisma couldn't keep the bubble of anger from rising through Indigo's body.

'*Really?*' she spluttered, taking a step back to run a critical gaze over his long, lean body.

'You're *really* going to take the room when you can plainly see that *I was here first*!'

He turned to look at her again, his expression giving nothing away as his heavy-lidded gaze swept over her face.

She felt exposed, almost naked under his scrutiny, and had to fight not to wrap her arms around her body for protection against it. Locking her jaw, she stared him out, knowing from experience that not backing down was the only way she was going to get what she wanted. Or, in this case, what she needed—a comfortable bed for the night. Which had already been paid for!

A muscle twitched in the Frenchman's jaw as he kept his gaze fixed on hers. He really did have the most striking face, with prominent high-set cheekbones and a broad masculine brow above those mesmerising eyes. What was it about French men that made them so unutterably sexy? The ones she'd met throughout her life had all had the same confident, direct gaze that made her feel simultaneously appraised and giddily unnerved. It was as though he was scrutinising the whole of her exterior whilst also looking deep inside her.

The feeling of being so thoroughly examined made her whole body tingle.

She stared harder at him to combat her dip in concentration.

Something flashed in his eyes and the corner of his mouth lifted fractionally. Was he amused by her determination to win?

Scowling as frustration pricked at her skin, she opened her mouth to restate her case—but he beat her to it.

'You're right,' he said bluntly. 'You must have the room.'

Indigo blinked at him in surprise, snapping her mouth shut. This, she had not expected.

'Oh! Okay.' She frowned, a little dazed by how easy that had been. 'Really?'

Sighing, he ran a hand over his clean-shaven jaw. 'To be honest, *mademoiselle*, I'm too tired to argue. It's been—' he winced, his expression turning troubled '—an *intense* day for me and I want to relax before starting my walk tomorrow.'

'Wait—you're walking the coast too?' she asked in surprise. Looking at him, standing there in his expensive suit with his designer bags sitting prettily at his feet, she'd imagined he was here to do some upmarket sightseeing in the town, or perhaps conduct a high-powered business meeting in the hotel.

His eyes crinkled at the corners as he half frowned, half smiled. 'Is that so unlikely?' he asked, his voice tinged with playful irony.

The bottom fell out of her stomach. 'No! No, I guess not.'

'Anyway, what kind of a man would I be to leave a lady stranded in a strange town in the middle of the night?'

Something about the way he said this, with a twist of wry humour, stopped her from telling him she didn't need a *man's* help—that she'd managed perfectly well on her own for the last three months without one, despite the challenges she'd faced.

'But, *Signor*, there are no other rooms available in Amalfi!' the receptionist cut in before Indigo could form a reply. 'It's a busy time and all the hotels in the town are booked up. I know this because I've already phoned around for another traveller.'

The Frenchman turned to face her. 'You're telling me you can't find me an alternative room for the night?' he stated with unnerving calm.

She shrank away from his gaze, suddenly seeming a lot less self-assured than she had a few minutes ago. 'Yes, *Signor*, I'm so sorry,' she said, her swallow appearing to catch in her throat. 'I'll be able to give you the suite you booked from tomorrow, but tonight there aren't any other rooms available—'

'This is unacceptable,' he said quietly, but with a girder of steel to his voice. 'I do not expect this level of incompetence from an establishment like this. Fetch your manager.'

The receptionist's shoulders tensed as if she'd balled her fists and her eyes widened. 'I can't disturb him—he is sleeping right now and has given strict instructions not to be woken—'

'I don't care. Get him.' He leant forward, pressing his hands against the desk. 'Now.'

'Please, *Signor*, I'll lose my job,' she whispered. 'I'm new here and I can't afford to make any mistakes.' Her brow tensed as her eyes took on a look of abject panic.

The desperation in her voice made Indigo's stomach tighten as a wave of pity washed over her. She could see by the way the young woman's eyes had pooled with impending tears that she was both terrified of her boss and totally inexperienced in dealing with this level of cold assertiveness from a customer.

'Describe the suite to me,' Indigo blurted to the receptionist before the Frenchman could respond.

The receptionist turned to stare at her in surprise before recovering quickly, using the question as a lifeline to pull her professional self back to safety. 'There is a beautifully appointed bedroom with a super king-sized bed and an en suite bathroom—'

'Does the bedroom door have a lock?' Indigo asked.

Out of the corner of her eye she saw the Frenchman turn to stare at her in baffled disbelief. She ignored him.

'Yes, *Signorina*,' the receptionist replied, looking confused to have her patter broken into with such an odd question, 'and the separate living area has the latest entertainment system—'

'And a large sofa?' Indigo cut in again.

The receptionist blinked hard and frowned, then her expression softened with a mixture of relief and gratitude as she realised where Indigo was going with this. This time she didn't falter with her answer. 'Absolutely! It is very comfortable—large enough to fully stretch out on. There is also a separate bathroom with a whirlpool tub and a waterfall shower.'

Indigo nodded decisively. 'Okay then, we'll share it.'

'What?' The word jumped from the Frenchman's mouth as if he'd not been able to stop it.

She took a breath and turned to face his incredulous gaze. 'I'll take the sofa in the living room, you can have the bedroom; that way we both get to sleep tonight.'

The Frenchman's brow crinkled in disdain. '*Non*. Thank you, but I don't think that's appropriate.'

She raised an eyebrow. 'I don't bite, you know.'

His mouth twisted into a wry smile. 'I'm sure you don't, but it seems improper to ask you to share your room with a strange man.'

'You don't seem that strange to me.' She cast him a smile, which he begrudgingly returned, one eyebrow raised.

'But, seriously, it's fine,' she said. 'I don't mind sharing and I'd hate to feel responsible for this woman losing her job.'

He flapped his hand, dismissing her concern. 'It wouldn't be your fault.'

She looked him hard in the eye. 'But I'd still blame myself and it would ruin my holiday. Anyway, it doesn't sound like you have a better option.'

He gave a gentle snort and shook his head, wearily rubbing his hand over his forehead, as he appeared to give her suggestion some serious consideration. 'Are you sure you're happy to do this?' he asked, his eyes dark with indecision.

'Yes, of course!' she said brightly. 'When life throws problems at you, you have to do whatever you can to make the best of a situation.' She produced a firm smile. 'Anyway, what kind of a *woman* would I be to send an exhausted man out into the night to sleep on the streets in such a beautiful designer suit?'

He looked at her intently for another few seconds, as if giving her the chance to change her mind, and when she resolutely kept her mouth shut he gave a sharp nod.

'Okay, but you take the bedroom so you can lock the door; that way you have no reason to feel unsafe. I'll take the sofa. I'll be up and out early in the morning so I won't be in your way.' Without waiting for her response, he bent down to scoop up his luggage.

'I'm getting up early myself,' she said to the top of his head, her cheeks heating a little as she realised how defiant that sounded. For some reason she didn't want him to think she was some kind of lazy slob.

'Then we'll each have to pretend the other doesn't exist,' he said with a flash of droll humour in his eyes as he looked back up at her, pushing a hand through his hair as he righted himself.

An impossible feat, Indigo thought, her eyes following the movement of his long fingers and the way his hair fell perfectly back into place, as if it didn't dare defy him. There was no way a man like this could ever be ignored.

Turning back to the receptionist, he held out

his passport. 'If you'll give us two key cards we'll find our own way up to the room.'

With an air of sombre apology, the receptionist checked the passport, then picked up Indigo's—which was still lying on the reception desk—and tapped something into her computer. After swiping a couple of key cards through a machine, she handed everything back to the Frenchman. 'There are extra blankets and pillows in the wardrobes. I hope you will be comfortable,' she said sheepishly, before scurrying away to serve someone who had just arrived at the other end of the desk.

Handing Indigo her passport and key card, he turned abruptly on his heel and, without another word, strode away from her, bags swinging from his hand.

Clearly he was a leader, not a follower.

Indigo paused for a moment, staring after him, suddenly feeling a little unsure of herself.

Had she really just offered to share a suite with a complete stranger?

She was so used to figuring out quick fixes at work it hadn't struck her exactly what she'd committed to until it was too late to back out of it.

As she watched him reach the elevator and jab the button to call it, exhaustion from the mad scramble to get her community café in good shape so she didn't have to worry about it whilst she was away hit her like a wallop to the gut. The last three months had been tough, filled with worry about whether the funding she'd applied for in order to keep it running would materialise, and it all seemed to be catching up with her now.

Ironically, this week away was supposed to be a break from the stress of it. Initially it had struck her as ridiculous to come on holiday when she had the possibility of losing everything hanging over her head, but she'd dropped the ball and made a few silly mistakes recently that, while fixable, had meant she'd cost the café some money it could ill afford. As her friend

Lacey had jokingly pointed out, it would probably do both her and the café some good to have some time apart.

Added to which, all the travel and accommodation for this week had already been paid for and was non-refundable, so it would have been a waste of money *not* to come.

Wastage was something she felt very strongly about.

Anyway, it was too late to change her mind now—even if she let the Frenchman have the suite to himself. She didn't have the money to pay for a room in another hotel, let alone the energy to face the monumental task of finding one.

This was her only option.

Hurrying after him, she caught him up just as the elevator door opened with a smooth *swish*.

'Okay, let's do this,' she said, her words coming out a little breathlessly after her dash across the room.

He just smiled in a perplexed sort of way that made the skin prickle on the back of her neck, and gestured for her to walk into the elevator before him.

'No, no, after you,' she said, sweeping her own hand in an exaggerated arc towards the centre of the car.

Shaking his head in amusement, he stepped inside and moved to the back to allow her plenty of room to follow him in.

Once she was safely past the doors, he hit the button for their floor and the doors closed on them with another gentle *swish*.

Heavy silence fell between them.

Indigo shifted from one foot to the other.

Well, this is awkward.

'Perhaps we should introduce ourselves, since we're going to be suite-mates,' she said, raising a questioning eyebrow at him. 'I'm Indigo. Indigo Hughes.'

'Julien Moreaux,' he replied, catching her off guard by stepping forwards and kissing her gently on both cheeks.

Being English, she'd forgotten about this traditional French greeting and almost jumped away in shock, only managing to hold her nerve at the last second. His scent hit her nose again, even more intensely this time due to his proximity, and instinctively she breathed him in, intuiting cool nights after hot days, the crisp tang of cold wine in the sunshine and the musky scent of warm skin.

Delicious.

After he'd stepped back it took her a full couple of seconds to pull herself together again. She gave him a friendly smile, but what she really wanted to do was pull him back towards her, bury her face in the scoop of his neck and drag his scent deep into her lungs again.

What was wrong with her? She'd never had this kind of visceral response to a complete stranger before, but there was something so commanding about this man. He made her feel safe, somehow.

Oh, get a grip, Indigo!

The honeymoon suite was exquisite, decorated

in those amazing heritage colours that Italians employed so effortlessly, the furniture simple but refined, with an art deco theme tying the room together. Romantic aspiration seemed to ooze from the walls, as if they'd been infused with the happiness of all the newlyweds that had stayed there over the years. She felt sure this place had to have been included in every *World's Best Honeymoon Suites* article written for the glossy magazines she judiciously avoided buying these days.

After thoroughly investigating the suite with her eyes, she turned to look at Julien and realised that he hadn't even glanced around him and was instead staring down at the screen of his phone.

Clearly he was already *au fait* with the finer things in life.

Shaking her head at his lack of interest, she went to explore the bedroom, which was just as overwhelmingly beautiful as the rest of the suite. This whole experience was like stepping into a fantasy.

Despite her protests about it being a waste of money, Gavin, her ex, had insisted on booking the first night of their stay in this expensive hotel—he'd wanted to start the holiday in style—before spending the rest of the week moving between smaller, more basic places. So this would be her only chance for luxurious pampering.

She was going to have to make the most of it.

After grabbing a blanket and pillow for Julien from the wardrobe, she floated back out of the bedroom and dumped them on the sofa before turning to find he was still staring down at his phone, lost in his own world.

'Stay in the honeymoon suite a lot, do you?' she asked, edging her voice with dry amusement.

He glanced up at her and for a split second a dark expression flickered across his face. 'Only once.'

His change in demeanour unsettled her. 'You're married?' she asked to cover her discomfort.

'Not any more.'

She could have sworn the temperature dropped a few degrees.

'Oh. Sorry to hear that.'

He flipped her his teasing grin again, breaking the tension. 'You English are always sorry for something.'

'I was just being polite,' she said, bristling.

His grin deepened.

She cocked an eyebrow back at him.

He looked at her for a moment longer with amusement in his eyes before turning away to drop his bags next to a mosaic-tiled coffee table in the middle of the room. 'Well, I'm going to— what do you English say?—*crash out*,' he said.

That was her cue to leave. And not a moment too soon. Her whole body felt hot and tingly with the awareness of being alone with him.

'Me too,' Indigo said, backing towards the bedroom. 'So I guess I won't see you in the morning.'

'Probably not,' he said, flopping down on to the sofa and stretching his arms above his head.

She came to a halt in the doorway and watched with fascination as he put everything he had into the stretch, the pleasure of it rippling across his face as he released the tension in his muscles. Forcing herself not to run her eyes up and down the powerful length of his body, she gave a stiff bob of her head, then turned to walk into the bedroom, shutting the door firmly behind her, pushing away the ridiculous urge to lie down on top of him—chest to chest, thigh to thigh—just to feel the solid strength of him beneath her.

It brought it home to her how much she'd missed being touched, being held, just being physically close to someone since Gavin had left her. Now she had the time and space to think about it, the after-effects seemed to be coming out in the strangest of ways.

She turned the key decisively in the lock, hearing it click.

Flinging herself at Julien was definitely not the way to deal with things.

Okay, time to put the sexy Frenchman out of her mind and get practical.

Striding purposefully away from the door, she dropped the small rucksack she'd used as hand luggage on to the bed. Thank goodness she'd had the forethought to pack a few essentials into it for just such an occurrence.

Even so, after spending a lot of time planning for this trip, it was unnerving to find herself without all her carefully thought-out trekking gear. She didn't even have her walking boots with her, so she would have to walk for at least five hours each day in the trainers she'd changed into at the last second at the airport because her feet were so hot. What an unfortunate decision that had been.

Hopefully the airline would find her bag soon and send it to one of the hotels on the route. She'd left her details and itinerary with the lost luggage desk at the airport and they'd promised—after what seemed like hours of form-filling—to send it on once it had been located.

The biggest problem she faced was that she'd put half of her money and her emergency credit card into the lost backpack too, not wanting to carry it all in her hand luggage in case that was stolen. At least her breakfasts were already paid for, so she could eat heartily in the morning and maybe skip lunch in order to eke out what little cash she had to feed herself in the evenings. Just until her backpack turned up. Which would be okay. She was used to budgeting and eating frugally.

It would all be part of the adventure.

Emptying out her rucksack on to the bed-spread, she took an inventory of what she had with her: one extra pair of knickers and one pair of socks—that she'd have to alternate with the ones she had on and wash each day—a tooth-brush and a tiny tube of toothpaste, a spare T-shirt and a short cotton skirt which she'd interchange with the shorts and vest she had on, a pack of mints, a mascara that promised to give you 'Hollywood eyes' and her trusty liquid eyeliner, a packet of painkillers, her wallet and passport and a book on walking the Amalfi coast. She didn't even have her mobile phone with her, she realised with a lurch, because she'd packed that into her missing luggage too, determined to only use it for emergencies on the trip so that she'd make the most of the scenery and social life and not be constantly diverted by the online world.

After packing everything carefully back into the bag, she took a refreshing shower in the floor-to-ceiling marble bathroom, lathering herself with the zingy-smelling complimentary shower gel, before sliding between the crisp cotton sheets of the bed.

What luxury!

Stretching herself into a starfish shape, she brushed her fingertips over the smooth mahogany headboard and sighed hard, painfully aware of how much empty space there was on either side of her.

The cruel irony of staying in the honeymoon suite had not been lost on her.

In a parallel universe—where Gavin hadn't fallen in love with another woman—she'd be tumbling into bed with him right about now.

What would he have said about staying in this room? She pictured them laughing about it, ribbing each other about how much sex they should be having to keep up with all the former inhabitants. Out of nowhere a feeling of utter desolation hit her right in the chest. It had been three months since they'd split up and she'd not allowed herself to fall apart since the day it had happened, keeping herself busy and using this holiday as a bright spot to look forward to when she felt glum. But the realisation that this was it—that she was here now, on her own, and this was the reality of her situation suddenly brought her low.

She thumped the mattress on either side of her. She was *not* going to let it get her down.

As she'd learnt from an early age, crying and

whinging didn't get you anywhere. That was what growing up in an all-male household and having four smart, alpha, and now highly successful older brothers would teach you. She'd never won an argument or topped a challenge by turning on the waterworks or asking for special dispensation, and that was the way she preferred it. Everything she'd achieved had been on her own merits. She'd fought just as hard—if not harder—than her brothers for her successes and she was proud of what she'd achieved.

Unfortunately, Gavin hadn't understood that drive to succeed on her own, and had cited her desire to pour too much time and energy into making her café a success and 'excluding him from parts of her life where he wasn't necessary' as the catalyst for their breakup. According to him, she treated him like one of her projects and acted as if she had more love for the strangers who frequented the café than for him. That had been particularly gutting to hear because she liked to think of herself as a perceptive and caring partner.

Pushing away the threatening gloom, she sat up and punched her pillows back into shape before flopping back down and wriggling further into the sumptuous bed.

Well, from this point on she was looking after herself.

Whilst she was here she was going to get some fresh air and exercise, meet people outside of her small sphere of work and recharge her batteries before returning home feeling refreshed and more positive about her future.

As she lay there, willing away the lingering tight feeling in her chest, something about her earlier head-to-head with Julien suddenly occurred to her. He'd conducted his whole conversation, even the bit with the receptionist, in English. Had he done that so as not to exclude her? Or was he just better at English than Italian? From her experience with him so far, she got the impression he'd be good at everything he did—he certainly exuded that kind of confidence.

Except for that moment when he'd talked about how *intense* his day had been. There had been a vulnerability to his voice that hadn't been there for the rest of the time.

Whatever could have affected him so deeply? Could it have something to do with his failed marriage?

Perhaps he, too, was here to get a new perspective on life after a bad breakup.

She knew first-hand how demoralising it could be going through a divorce. Gavin, her ex, had been an utter mess when he'd first moved into her spare room—which she'd offered to him as a favour to a friend of a friend after his wife demanded they separate. At that point it had been six months since her father had passed away and she was finding it very lonely living in their empty family home without him, so it had been nice to have the company.

She'd found comfort in taking care of Gavin:

making him healthy meals when she discovered he wasn't eating properly and sitting with him, listening to him talk through his pain and humiliation for hours and hours.

At the time, she hadn't anticipated it turning into a relationship, but there it was. In retrospect, it seemed inevitable now that something more would have developed between them, especially when they'd grown so emotionally close.

A prickle of disquiet ran up her spine.

She really should have asked Julien if he was okay when he'd mentioned his divorce. In her experience, whenever people brought up things like that it was usually because they wanted to talk to someone about it, but she'd blithely ignored his prompt, more concerned about rebutting his teasing. It was possible she could use her experience to help him out in some way, though. As one concerned human being to another. Considering he was here on his own, she wouldn't be surprised to find he didn't have anyone at home he could talk to about what he was going through.

Turning over and letting out a huge yawn, she told herself that if she saw Julien again on the walk she'd make an effort to check that he was okay, just to set her mind at rest. But that would be it. The whole experience with Gavin had made her very wary of getting romantically involved with a divorcee again—she never wanted to be someone's rebound relationship ever again.

So for now, she was going to put the sexy Frenchman—unnervingly close on the other side of the door—out of her mind.

CHAPTER TWO

The Ravello Circuit. A tricky walk with lots of steps. We recommend breaking the walk at the magnificent Villa Cimbrone gardens before visiting Ravello, then stopping for a scenic lunch break in Pontone...

JULIEN MOREAUX AWOKE to find the sun streaming in through the large windows of the honeymoon suite. He rubbed a hand across his bleary eyes, forcing his thoughts into some kind of coherent arrangement.

He was here, in Amalfi. Finally.

It hadn't mattered to him exactly where he'd end up when he'd asked his PA to book this break for him—all he'd stipulated was that he wanted somewhere where he could move from one place to another so he didn't feel trapped into having to see the same people in the same place every day—and he was pleased with her choice.

This walking holiday had been marked in his mind for some time as the beginning of the return to the way things used to be, and he'd been looking forward to losing himself in the monotony of hard exercise and self-imposed solitude.

Not that the solitude part had worked out well so far.

He grimaced as the events of the previous evening came back to haunt him. Sharing his suite with a bohemian idealist with an overblown zeal for life had not been an ideal start, but after sensing Indigo's desperation to fix the situation amicably and seeing the earnest pleading in her eyes, he'd known there was no way he could refuse her suggestion.

And he was tired of being the bad guy.

A huge yawn hit him and he rocked his head back against the soft cushions of the sofa, giving his body a long, hard stretch to wake up his cramped muscles.

Considering the way he was feeling this morning, he suspected, if he allowed himself, he could easily spend the whole week sleeping. Not that he was going to do that. He'd come here for a change of scene and a reprieve from the pressures of life and there was no way he was wasting his time in Italy staring at four walls. Even if they were as magnificent as the ones in this hotel.

This observation led his thoughts back to Indigo's wry comment about him being familiar with staying in the honeymoon suite.

A cold prickle ran across his skin.

The last time he'd been in a room like this he'd thought his life had been on the up and up, but look at him now, barely two years later, holidaying alone only hours after signing his divorce papers, with the ink of his signature still drying in his mind.

Swinging himself into a sitting position on the

sofa, he stifled another yawn behind his hand and rubbed his face hard to get the blood circulating.

He really needed to get up and out before Indigo emerged; he didn't think he had the mental energy this morning to deal with another awkward scene with her.

Glancing towards the bedroom door, he was surprised to see it standing wide open.

Huh, weird. He checked his watch. Seven o'clock. So she hadn't been joking when she said she'd be up and out early too.

Hauling himself off the sofa, he went to investigate further.

'Indigo?' he called gently, so as not to startle her in case she was still in there.

There was no reply.

Poking his head around the doorway, he saw that the bed was empty, with the sheets pulled haphazardly back and the door to the en suite bathroom flung open.

She was gone.

That was a relief.

Feeling the tension leave his shoulders, he went back into the living area and pulled out the clothes he was going to wear for his walk today, before heading off for an invigorating shower.

There had been something about her that intrigued him, though, he mused as he felt the soothing water cascade over his aching back—her determination and bolshie confidence perhaps. She certainly wasn't his usual type, with her leggy, voluptuous figure and short, feathery bobbed hair in a shocking shade of red, which had reminded him of the colour of the sea of poppy fields behind the house in Provence where he'd grown up. Historically, he'd always been attracted to petite women, usually blondes, with more of a delicate air about them, but there was something incredibly alluring about Indigo, with her wide, open smile and playful gaze.

She was sexy.

He shut off the water and reached for a towel, drying himself vigorously. If he was being honest, she'd probably only captured his interest because it had been refreshing to meet a woman who didn't want to take something from him and just walk away for once. He was used to being the one to sort out other people's problems, and it had been a long time since someone had done something benevolent for him.

It would be better if he didn't see her again, though, he told himself, flinging the towel into the bath. He wasn't in any state to be sociable at the moment.

After shaving off his morning stubble, he pulled on shorts, a light breathable T-shirt and the brand new walking boots that his PA had sourced for him, and gave himself a nod in the mirror.

Okay. Now he was ready to face the day and whatever it might bring.

He checked his email on his phone as he travelled down in the elevator ready to grab some breakfast in the restaurant, pleased to find there wasn't anything that needed his urgent attention. That was sure to change by the end of the week, though.

After dropping by the reception desk to confirm they'd have the suite that he'd booked available for him when he returned from his hike, he was about to walk away to get his breakfast when curiosity about Indigo's situation stopped him. He should probably check whether he was likely to come across her again, just so he could prepare himself for it.

He turned back.

'Did you find another room here for the woman I shared the honeymoon suite with last night?' he asked the receptionist.

Confusion flickered across her face, until recollection seemed to strike her. 'The lady from your suite checked out, *Signor.*'

That must mean she wasn't doing the Ravello circuit and coming back to Amalfi today, which meant there wasn't any danger of bumping into her again.

Good, that was good, because he'd feel compelled to acknowledge her if they saw each other again, which would encroach on his much anticipated alone time.

'Okay, thanks,' he said, giving the receptionist a nod before heading over to the breakfast room at the other end of the lobby.

Considering it was still pretty early, the place was already buzzing with guests, and he grabbed the only spare table near the back wall. After seating himself, he took a look around him, soaking up the animated vibe. Quite a few of the guests seemed to be dressed in walking gear, like him. Clearly the coastal walk was a big draw to the area. Hmm, perhaps it wouldn't be as solitary an experience as he was hoping, he reflected with a twinge of annoyance.

A flash of bright red on the other side of the room caught his eye and, heart thumping, he quickly leant back, using the couple sitting at the table next to him as cover. Grabbing the menu in front of him and holding it to hide most of his face, he gradually leant forwards again to take another look. As he suspected, it was Indigo, standing at the breakfast buffet with her back to him, her hair damp and gleaming and her small rucksack slung over one arm.

She looked refreshed and energised this morning, her skin glowing with health and her posture relaxed. His gaze followed her as she moved smoothly along the buffet, seemingly checking over her options before making her choice. She grabbed an apple and a couple of bread rolls from the display and he stared in baffled amusement as she slipped them into the gaping opening of her bag. After a quick check around, she seemed to discern that no one was watching her and popped a couple of slices of Parma ham and a small bottle of mineral water from the cooler section in there too. Next went in a pat of butter and a little package of cheese.

Evidently deciding she had enough food stashed away, she strolled nonchalantly away from the buffet, slinging her bag over her shoulder and shoving her hands deep into the pockets of her shorts. He half expected her to start whistling *Food, Glorious Food* as she made her getaway.

She was staying in a five-star hotel, but she was too cheap to buy her own lunch? What was that about?

He allowed himself one last look at her long, shapely legs as she disappeared out of the room, then turned to gesture for the waitress to bring him some coffee.

And that, he guessed, feeling an odd twinge in his chest, would probably be the last he'd ever see of Indigo Hughes.

Indigo had thought she was in pretty good shape. She went to the gym at least a couple of times a week and opted to walk around London as much as possible instead of jumping on public transport, but by the time she'd climbed what seemed like a thousand steps leading away from Amalfi—pausing on her journey to walk through the ancient brick-walled walkways hung with canopies of vibrant greenery in the Villa Cimbrone gardens—then on to the quaint little town of Ravello, she realised her fitness levels were nothing like as good as she'd imagined.

Still, she'd made it here without incident, and after wandering around the quiet streets crammed with cool artisan shops and visiting the simple but atmospheric cathedral, it was a relief to walk downhill to the little village of Pontone and stop for a rest and to eat her lunch.

Sitting on a wide grassy viewpoint which looked out over the dramatic drop down to the coast, she was just about to take the final bite of the sandwich she'd made out of the food she'd filched from the breakfast buffet when she noticed a familiar figure making his way across the grass in the direction of the *trattorias* that, according to her guide, were favoured by walkers on the route because of the incredible views from their balconies.

After spending the whole morning trying not to think about the sight of Julien lying bare-chested on the sofa, looking utterly divine in repose as she tiptoed past him, she was disconcerted to see him again in the flesh. Not that she was going to let that stop her from being friendly. She'd made that promise to herself to check he was okay here on his own, so that was what she was going to do. Just because he was ridiculously sexy and ever so slightly intimidating it didn't mean she couldn't have a friendly chat with him.

'Hi there,' she called as he came level with where she was sitting.

He didn't appear to hear her.

'Julien! Hey, Julien, over here!' she shouted this time. She could have sworn she saw him flinch before turning to look over to where she was sitting. He raised a hand and gave her a nod of acknowledgement, before turning back and continuing on his journey.

Huh.

Perhaps he assumed she wouldn't want to be

disturbed whilst eating her lunch. Yes, that must be it; he couldn't be deliberately avoiding her.

Could he?

No—she was being paranoid.

Jumping up and grabbing her daypack, she made after him, having to pick up her pace in order to catch up with him before he strode out of sight.

'Hey, Julien, wait!' she called, a little out of breath by the time she reached him.

He turned around and gave her a look of expectant concern. 'Are you okay?' he asked, his gaze flicking behind her as if he was worried she was being pursued.

'I'm fine,' she panted, 'just wanted to check you're enjoying your day. You seemed a little— er—' she flapped a hand at him '—stressed yesterday.'

He took a small step backwards and let out a sharp snort. 'Yes, I'm enjoying it so far.' A small frown flickered across his face. 'Thank you.'

There was a pause while she waited for him to ask if she was having a good time too.

He didn't.

'Okay, good.' She clapped her hands together awkwardly. 'Well, I just wanted to say hi. So, hi!' she blurted, sincerely hoping he'd assume the blush travelling up her neck was a flush from the sun and her mad dash across the grass.

'Hi,' he replied flatly, folding his arms across his chest.

There was another heavy pause where he blinked at her, as if waiting for her to make her excuses and leave. Well, she wasn't going to. She'd learnt over the last year whilst working at the café that just because someone seemed unfriendly when you first spoke to them, it didn't necessarily mean they didn't want to talk to you. They were probably just distracted by something they'd been thinking about, or they were hungry, or concerned about the tightness of their trousers or something. Not that it appeared as though any of his clothes weren't fitting him perfectly.

In fact, he looked as if he'd just stepped off a page in one of the hiking gear magazines she'd pored over whilst preparing for the holiday, before realising she could afford exactly none of the items in it.

'Did you like Ravello? All those steps up to it nearly killed me!' she joked, cringing inside at the hint of desperation in her voice.

He didn't even break a smile. 'Yes, it was an interesting place.' His brow creased into a frown. 'They told me at the reception desk you'd checked out. I didn't expect to see you on this circuit today.'

She stiffened, wondering why on earth he seemed so irritated about her walking the same route as him.

'I have another hotel in town booked for tonight. A better organised one, I hope,' she said, shrugging off her discomfort and forcing a smile on to her face.

'Okay. *Bon.*' He took a deliberate step backwards, then froze as her words seemed to sink in. 'Do you mean you're staying in Amalfi again tonight?'

Another wave of warmth began to creep up her neck. 'Yup.'

His brow crinkled in confusion. 'Then why are you moving hotels after only one night?'

She shifted uncomfortably. 'I like to change things up. It keeps me on my toes.'

And I can't afford to stay in that hotel again, not that I'm admitting that to you, Monsieur Moneybags.

He nodded slowly, his gaze searching hers as if he was trying to rootle out a lie.

She just raised both eyebrows at him, determined not to give in and blurt out the truth, trying to ignore the way her pulse had sped up.

Letting out a sharp huff of a laugh, Julien broke eye contact and glanced behind him as if looking for an excuse to leave. Not that she could blame him; the conversation wasn't exactly flowing well and she was tempted to slink away herself. But she wasn't going to; she was going to see this through to the bitter end, as a matter of personal fulfilment.

'So, are you going to try one of those *trattorias* for your lunch?' she pressed, nodding in the direction he'd been heading.

He closed his eyes for a second and pulled in a sharp breath, then smiled politely. '*Oui*. I didn't have the forethought to bring any food with me.' He gestured towards the remains of her sandwich, which was still clutched in her hand. 'Where did you get your lunch today?' The dry irony in his tone suggested there was more to his question than a simple polite query.

He must have seen her take the food from the buffet. The realisation sent a prickle up her spine. Normally she would never have done such a thing, hating the idea of stealing anything from anyone, but with the limited funds she had available until her bag turned up, it was necessary to bend her rules a little.

'I purloined it from the breakfast buffet,' she admitted, forcing herself to keep her chin up and her gaze locked with his. 'I thought the least the hotel could do was gift me a lunch after their mess-up with the room last night. Anyway, a place like that always puts out more than is consumed. I was helping with their wastage problem,' she finished, aware that her tone was edged with defensiveness.

His eyes crinkled at the corners as his wry smile deepened. 'Don't worry; your secret is safe with me,' he murmured, leaning closer and enveloping her in his delicious scent.

It was all she could do not to take a great gulping breath of it through her nose. What was it that made his smell so enticing to her? Was this what people called the pheromone effect? She'd never experienced it before.

'Thanks,' she deadpanned.

He gave her a curt nod. 'Well, I'm going to go and eat.'

'Okay, enjoy,' she said, disappointed that he was leaving now. Despite his standoffishness, she'd enjoyed chatting with him after spending her morning alone. All the other English-speaking walkers she'd encountered on the route seemed to be part of a group, which she hadn't had the courage to try and break into yet.

She watched him stride away, trying not to stare at the way he moved his large, fit body with such powerful grace.

Judging by his troubled mood, she guessed he must be struggling with some serious emotional turmoil, which she knew from personal experience could make for a pretty lonely existence. She hated to see people in pain, especially if she thought she could do something to help.

Well, she'd just have to keep an eye out for him, just in case he fancied some no-strings company later.

CHAPTER THREE

Back in Amalfi. Make sure you take advantage of the wonderful selection of restaurants and eateries after visiting the imposing cathedral in the centre of the town...

AFTER THOROUGHLY ENJOYING the solitude of his walk earlier in the day, Julien had been looking forward to finding a place to grab a peaceful lunch when Indigo had run over and accosted him.

It had taken everything he'd had not to be rude and pretend he hadn't heard her calling out to him, then continue with their stilted conversation when it became clear she wasn't going to let him get away without extracting some kind of information out of him.

He wasn't sure why she'd been so keen to chat.

Perhaps she was lonely and hadn't found any other English speakers to buddy up with. He hoped she'd got the message that he preferred to holiday on his own now though, and wouldn't bother coming over to talk to him should their paths cross again.

A niggle of shame twisted in his gut. He felt bad about being so unfriendly, but she'd picked the wrong time to try and get to know him.

If that had been her objective.

Perhaps she was looking for something more. If that was the case, she was bang out of luck. After the train wreck of his marriage, he wanted nothing to do with women and relationships again for a very long time.

Even spirited ones with legs that went on for miles and eyes you could get lost in.

When he got back to the hotel, he took a long cooling shower then a refreshing nap before striking out for dinner, strolling through the centre of Amalfi on the way to the restaurants on the marina that the hotel receptionist had recommended he try.

Diverted by the magnificence of the *Duomo* in the town centre, he climbed the wide steps and walked through the Arabic style Cloister of Paradise, looking out through the grand archways at the panoramic view of the town, with its pastel-coloured stone buildings wrapped with iron balconies.

He knew what he was looking at should have blown him away, but ever since his life had fallen to pieces he'd had trouble finding pleasure in things. He felt desensitised to beauty, as if he was viewing it from inside a plastic bubble. Nothing seemed to touch him any more.

Shaking off the building tension at the base of his skull, he was just about to turn and walk back to the steps when a bright flash of red caught his eye.

Was that Indigo again?

Craning his neck, he tried to see past a crowd of tourists blocking his view and catch another glimpse of her so he could make sure to walk in the opposite direction, but she seemed to have disappeared. Was his brain playing tricks on him? No, it must have been her. That hair colour was so unusual it couldn't be someone else with the exact same shade—and he knew for a fact she was staying in Amalfi tonight.

Walking slowly down the steps, he forced himself to take a deep breath and relax, telling himself it was unlikely they'd cross each other's paths when it was so busy.

Reaching the Popolo fountain in the middle of the piazza, he sat down on the stone edge of it and ran his fingers through the water, enjoying the cooling effect on his skin. What was wrong with him today? His heart seemed to be racing and his palms felt sweaty.

The heat must be getting to him.

Someone sat down next to him and on impulse he glanced round to see who it was.

'Fancy seeing you here,' Indigo said, with a mischievous lift of her eyebrow.

He snorted and shook his head at his terrible luck. What was it about this woman that kept drawing them together?

'It's a small town centre; I guess we were bound to bump into each other at some point,' he said wearily.

She leant back on her hands and studied him. 'Are you off to forage for some supper?'

He raised his eyebrows, bemused. 'Forage?'

'Looking for a place to eat.'

'Oui.'

'On your own?'

'Oui.' He tensed, anticipating what was coming next.

'You're welcome to join me if you'd like,' she said brightly, confirming his fear. 'I was just about to grab a slice of pizza at one of those small family-run eateries just off the square.'

'You mean the cafés with the plastic tables? *Non*—' he began to say, but she cut him off.

'You'd be doing me a favour,' she said. 'I've been on my own all day and I'm beginning to have conversations with myself out loud, which is never a good sign. If you don't come and have dinner with me there's a good chance I'll be arrested by the end of the night and taken to a secure facility.' She sat up and folded her arms. 'Anyway, you owe me.'

He frowned, perplexed. 'What for?'

'For letting you share my room.'

'*Your* room?'

'I was there first, remember?'

He sighed, fighting a smile. 'How could I forget?'

'So what do you say? Can I tempt you with a slice of pizza?' She looked so hopeful it made something twist in his chest. But he needed to stay strong.

'I'm going to try out one of the restaurants down on the marina,' he said, giving her an apologetic look. 'Apparently they have fantastic à la carte menus with a good selection of locally caught fresh fish and seafood. Word has it the lobster spaghetti is not to be missed.'

Her eyes seemed to glaze over as if she was picturing the food he'd described. 'Sounds awful,' she joked, flashing an impertinent grin. 'Anyway, those places are a total tourist rip-off.'

'And the pizza joints aren't?'

Spreading out her hands, she gestured around the square. 'They're part of the local colour. You can eat overpriced gourmet food in Paris, or wherever you're from. Come and support the underdog for once.' She stared at him hard, like she'd done the previous night, dipping her head to one side and looking up at him through her thick black lashes, and something twisted again inside him—then broke.

Despite his earlier determination to keep to himself tonight, he realised he had no choice but to go and eat a huge greasy slice of pizza with this woman. Maybe then she'd leave him alone.

'Sure.' He threw up his hands in surrender. 'Pizza sounds good.'

'Great!' she said, breaking into a huge smile.

He hoped she wasn't going to read too much

into this. Whilst he was prepared to spend the next hour with her, he didn't want her thinking he wanted to buddy up for the whole week.

As they walked away from the piazza towards one of the back streets that housed the pizza outlets, they passed a homeless person slumped on a filthy-looking rug next to one of the souvenir shops. Out of the corner of his eye, he saw Indigo reach into her pocket, then discreetly drop a handful of coins into an empty hat by the side of the man, before strolling on as if nothing had happened.

As soon as they'd ordered their slices of pizza and drinks from a very jolly waiter at a café with red plastic tables and chairs arranged out on the pavement, Indigo excused herself and went inside to find the bathroom and splash some cool water on to her face.

Maybe insisting on bringing Julien here had been a little extreme, she deliberated as she patted her face dry with a paper towel. He'd not exactly been enthusiastic about taking her up on the offer of company—but she couldn't shake the concern that it would have been a miserable experience for him, eating dinner on his own, and she was pretty sure if she was patient he'd thaw out eventually.

Sometimes people put up barriers for whatever reason and you had to coax them out of their shell. She'd seen it a lot throughout her time running her café and evening classes. People could appear to be confident on the outside, but when you dug a little deeper it became apparent they were dealing with some tough issues and putting a brave face on things. Often they just needed someone to ask if they were okay, then listen to them.

Which was exactly what she'd done for Gavin, she remembered with a lurch. Not that he'd appreciated it in the end.

Sighing, she rubbed a hand over her face. Was she setting herself up for more trouble here, getting involved in Julien's drama?

She stared into the mirror, looking deep into her own eyes. No. Because this wasn't going to turn into anything more than a brief encounter—hopefully just one of many connections she'd make during her week here. She was here to socialise and have fun, new experiences this week after all, but that was all it would be.

Pulling a face at herself, she smoothed down her hair then pushed back her shoulders, wishing she'd had something other than her walking clothes to put on tonight. It wasn't that she wanted to impress Julien exactly, but she felt scruffy next to his overt sophistication, and less confident because of it.

Returning to the table, she saw that the waiter had brought their slices of pizza, as well as a beer for Julien and a glass of tap water for her.

Julien looked so strikingly out of place—sitting there on his cherry-red plastic chair in his designer jeans and beautifully cut open-necked shirt, with his golden hair swept back from his face and aviator sunglasses perched on his head as he read something on his smartphone—that she couldn't help but smile.

Taking her seat, she gave him a friendly nod as he looked up to acknowledge her return.

'Great, the food arrived while I was away; I love it when that happens,' she said, picking up her glass and taking a sip of water to cover a sudden bout of nerves at being there with him.

He just looked at her as if she was slightly loopy.

Swallowing hard, she put her glass down and leaned forwards, propping her arms on the table. 'So, tell me, Julien, why did you choose to walk the Amalfi coast?' she asked brightly in an attempt to get the conversation started.

He took his sunglasses off his head and slid them on to his nose so all she could see now was her own reflection in the lenses. 'It seemed like a good place to get away from it all.'

'Apart from all the tourists.' She gave him a smile, which he didn't return.

'I didn't realise how popular this place was.'

'You mean you didn't do your homework? Somehow I find that hard to believe,' she said.

He frowned. 'Really? Why?'

'I don't know… You just seem very—*together*. Very—*businesslike*.'

He huffed out a dry laugh and picked up his beer bottle, taking a long pull. 'Why did you choose to come here?' he asked, gesturing to their surroundings with the neck of the bottle.

She paused, arranging her answer in her mind. 'I've wanted to do this walk for ages and I finally got round to booking it this year,' she said, uncomfortably aware of a jolt of sadness in her chest. She and Gavin had talked about coming here since they'd got together, when things had been good between them. Before he'd started to resent her.

Julien leant back in his seat and studied her. 'Do you often holiday alone?'

'No, just this time.' She took a breath, deciding she might as well be straight with him.

'Actually, I was supposed to come here with

my boyfriend, but we split up three months ago. He didn't want to come with his new partner, so I figured, since it was non-refundable, I may as well use it as a chance to get away for a bit.' She was aiming for a breezy and upbeat tone of voice, but from the look on Julien's face she suspected she must have fallen well short.

Still, perhaps her confession would open up an opportunity for him to talk about his own situation.

'How about you? Were you supposed to come here with someone?' she asked, perhaps a little desperately.

He avoided her gaze, looking instead at the waiter who was busying about nearby. *'Non,'* was all he said, picking up his slice of pizza and taking a large bite.

'Oh.' She tapped her toe gently against the plastic leg of the table, then picked up her own slice and studied it, uncomfortably aware that she'd lost her appetite now.

'Well, it's really nice to be here, anyway,' she

continued, to cover the now rather prickly silence. 'I haven't had a holiday in a couple of years—if you don't count the four days I spent at my oldest brother's house over Christmas, which wasn't exactly a relaxing break. Three of my brothers have kids—one of them has four boys—so it was more like staying in a soft play gym crossed with a zoo.'

Picking up his beer, Julien took another long pull. 'You don't have your own kids?' he asked.

There was a sharp spasm in her chest. She'd fantasised about her and Gavin having kids, once upon a time. Another thing to mourn the loss of. 'Not yet. Hopefully one day. I'm sure it'll happen when it's the right time.'

He grimaced as if he had a bad taste in his mouth. 'The right time,' he repeated flatly.

'Yeah, I firmly believe that kids turn up when you most need them to.'

Looking over the top of his sunglasses, he gave her a withering stare.

Irritation pricked at her skin. 'So I'm guessing you don't have kids either?' she asked, determined to ignore his negativity.

'*Non.*' The word was terse and had a definite full stop at the end.

'But you'd like to, one day?'

'Can we change the subject?' he said levelly, but with an undertone of steel.

'Um, sure.' Clearly she'd hit a nerve.

Perhaps it was for the best that they talk about something else anyway. The subject wasn't exactly an inspiring one for her now that she was single.

Indigo nibbled at the crust of her pizza while she thought of a new topic of conversation.

'Your English is very good. Where do you live?'

'In Paris, but I conduct a lot of business in the English language.'

'Oh, yeah?'

For the first time that night he seemed to relax, pushing his sunglasses up on to his head again and sitting back in his chair. '*Oui.* My business acquires and renovates high-end holiday homes in France for clients all over the world. We also source and maintain corporate Parisian apartments for executives to live in whilst they conduct business in France.'

'Nice.'

'I enjoy it.'

'Lucrative.'

'Oui.'

'Good for you.'

'What about you? What do you do?' He took another large bite of his pizza.

'I run a café that uses mostly surplus and past *best before date* food from supermarkets and restaurants. We sell affordable meals for people on low incomes so they can come and get a square meal at least a couple of times a week. Since we opened, we've had a lot of elderly gentlemen come in who've lost their wives and have no idea how to cook, so I started running cookery lessons in the evenings aimed specifically at people like them, to give them a grounding in making basic, healthy meals for themselves at home. It's going well so far, but it's been hard work. We rely a lot on donations and public grants so there's loads of form filling and face-to-face negotiating, and quite a bit of pleading on bended knee.'

She took a large bite of her food to punctuate her monologue, not wanting to think about what would happen to the café if the next lot of funding didn't come through.

'I imagine you're very good at the negotiating part,' he said with a twist in his smile.

'Usually,' she said through a mouthful of pizza, smiling back at him with her eyes. It felt good to finally hit on a subject he wanted to talk about.

'It's hard work to keep a project like that adequately funded, though. There's a constant threat of grants being pulled or reduced, so I spend a lot of my time looking for new sources of cash. It's hand to mouth in every way, but we make it work.'

'Did you set it up by yourself?' The last of his pizza disappeared into his mouth.

'Initially, but I have a dedicated team of both paid workers and local volunteers now.' She took another bite of her own food, aware that she needed to eat quickly now to catch up.

'That's impressive. No wonder you need a holiday.'

'Yeah, I've put in some very long days this past year. It's never going to make me rich, but it makes me happy.' At least it had, until her relationship with Gavin ended because of it.

Julien studied her again, this time with a small pinch between his brows.

'What?' she asked, swiping at her chin, worried that she had cheese strings dangling from it.

'I was just thinking it's good to meet someone with such drive and ambition.'

She smiled back in gratified surprise, feeling warmth pool in her belly. Putting her food back on the plate, she wiped her greasy fingers on the paper napkin next to it. 'Thanks. I've always wanted to run my own business—I hate the idea of working for other people for my entire life.' She took a breath. 'I think I was meant to do what I do.'

He snorted gently. 'You're a strong believer in fate. I suppose you're one of those people who think everything happens for a reason?'

'Sure am.' She stared at her pizza, wondering whether she could force down another bite. 'You've just got to keep positive and everything will work itself out in the end.'

When she looked up at him she was disturbed to see his expression had switched to a mixture of amusement and derision.

She frowned, riled by his change in attitude. 'What's so wrong with that?'

He shrugged and stared off into the distance. 'It's total claptrap.' He enunciated the word *claptrap* with some relish.

'It's not claptrap. It's called having a constructive outlook on life.'

Julien grunted and took another long sip of his beer. 'I suppose you believe in fairy tales too.'

'You must believe in happy-ever-afters if you got married,' she pointed out.

His gaze snapped back to hers. 'Maybe. Once. But divorce will knock that kind of naivety right out of you.'

She jumped as he thumped his beer bottle down on to the table between them, and there was an edgy pause as the word 'divorce' buzzed in the air between them like an irritating fly.

'Why did the two of you split up?' she asked gently, relieved they were finally getting to the crux of the matter.

He sighed and folded his arms. 'You know, I don't really want to talk about it. I came on this walk to forget about what went wrong in my life and look forward to a future on my own.' He over-enunciated the word 'own' this time.

Indigo bristled at his bluntness. 'That sounds kind of lonely.'

'Lonely sounds pretty good to me right now.'

The hollow look in his eyes disturbed her.

'You know, if you *did* want to talk about it, I'd be happy to listen,' she said.

His expression flashed with exasperation. 'I don't need some *amateur* psychoanalysing me this week, thanks.'

The stab of hurt she experienced must have shown on her face, because he gave a guttural sigh and shook his head.

Pushing his chair back from the table, he stood up and pulled a handful of notes out of his pocket, tossing them on to the table. 'I don't think I'm the kind of company you're looking for right now, Indigo,' he said tersely, dropping his glasses back down to cover his eyes. 'It's better if we don't spend any more time together. Enjoy the rest of your vacation.'

Without even glancing back, he strode away, his shoulders hunched and his arms hanging stiffly by his sides.

The whole surface of her skin felt hot and

prickly with indignation as she stared after him, his words echoing cruelly through her head.

How rude! She'd just wanted to check he was okay here on his own.

Not feeling lost and alone and isolated.

But okay. Fine! If that was the way he wanted it she wouldn't bother trying to be friendly any more.

Swallowing down the painful lump in her throat, she rummaged around in her bag for her purse.

What was wrong with her? She didn't seem to be able to step away from other people's problems, even on holiday.

She shouldn't be spending her precious free time with someone who had such a cynical view about love either, she told herself, yanking the money out of the notes compartment. She needed to surround herself with positivity and optimism right now.

Slamming her money down on the table next to his, she got up from her chair, set her shoulders back and walked in the opposite direction of the one he'd taken.

From this point on she would do as he asked and make a concerted effort to avoid any further contact with Monsieur Julien Moreaux.

CHAPTER FOUR

On to Praiano. A tough day's walk and the first leg of your journey west...

JULIEN KNEW HE shouldn't have kept on drinking after leaving Indigo at the table, but he'd needed to do something to numb the mortification that had trickled through him like ice water when he thought about how bitter and miserable he'd sounded. The look of hurt on her face after his blunt rejection of her offer of friendship had stayed imprinted on his mind's eye till he'd finally managed to wash it away with his fourth beer.

This was exactly why he'd decided to spend the week on his own. The last thing he'd wanted was to let his frustration over the failure of his marriage ruin the first proper break he'd had in a very long time, let alone affect someone else's holiday.

He took another long pull on his water bottle as he slogged along the rocky coastal path towards Praiano, willing the throbbing pain behind his eyes to dissipate. Because of his hangover, he'd started the walk later than he'd intended, and was paying for it now by having to trek hard through the midday sun to make up for the time he'd lost.

According to the hotel receptionist, there should be a small *tratorria* about an hour's walk from where he was. He was looking forward to eating a nourishing, carb-heavy meal to pick him up and give him the boost of energy he needed to get through the rest of the journey.

He attempted to while away the time by thinking through the next stages of a new build he'd been overseeing before coming here but, to his chagrin, Indigo's hurt expression kept popping back into his head. The worst thing, he finally accepted as he struggled along, was that he'd found himself beginning to like her as she'd revealed more about herself—particularly when she'd talked with such passion about the café and cooking classes she'd set up to cater for vulnerable members of her community.

He couldn't help but compare her to his ex-wife Celine, who, without even discussing it with him, had given up her job as a legal secretary as soon as they were married, spending her days shopping and watching reality TV instead. He'd not made a fuss at the time, thinking she'd probably grow bored after a while, but she hadn't. Instead, she'd looked to him to provide all her entertainment and society, as well as supporting her financially.

Which had been fine for a time.

After years of having his nose to the grindstone and putting his business ventures before his personal happiness, meeting the beautiful, wild and carefree Celine had been like being caught up in a cyclone of desire, and his formerly work-orientated life had suddenly become a whirl of new experiences and unpredictable passionate moments.

Until the bad luck that had changed everything for them, and his once happy-go-lucky wife turned into someone he didn't recognise any more.

Pushing against the surge of discontent that continued to live within him, forever threatening to pull him under, he strode on, picking up his pace as the *trattoria* finally swung into view.

He trudged up the steps to the seating area inside, now desperate for some shade and sustenance, and managed to secure a small table near the door, slumping into the chair with a sigh of relief.

A loud squall of laughter floated over from the other side of the restaurant, and he turned around to see what was going on.

There was a large group of walkers all crowded around a table at the back, which heaved with the remains of what had obviously been a hearty lunch.

The only person who didn't have a large empty plate in front of her, but was instead nursing a glass of what looked like water, was Indigo. She was talking animatedly with a ruddy-cheeked middle-aged man sitting next to her, and the rest of the group were leaning in, listening to the story she was telling. There was another roar of laughter as she concluded her tale, and she sat back with a wide, captivating smile on her face, then drained the last of her drink and stood up.

His eyes were immediately drawn to her long, shapely legs as she stepped back from the table, and his heart rate picked up as his mutinous mind conjured up the impression of how they might feel wrapped around him.

He turned away quickly as she went to grab her bag, not wanting her to catch him watching her, aware of a heavy pull of disgust with himself in the pit of his belly.

What was he doing? This was ridiculous. He wasn't going to cower here like an idiot. He looked up as she walked past his table, readying himself to face the music, but she didn't notice him sitting there, her eyes looking a little glazed as she made for the door.

Had she eaten anything since breakfast? He suspected not, judging by what he'd just witnessed, and now she was about to walk for another few hours in the hottest part of the day.

He shifted in his seat, irritated by her foolhardiness, aware of an achy tension in his body. Not that it was any of his concern. She was a grown woman who could fend for herself. If she weren't, surely she wouldn't have come on this walking holiday alone?

Except that she wasn't supposed to.

The thought gave him pause.

But no, she'd made the decision to come on her own and just because they'd shared an association, it didn't mean he should feel responsible for her well-being.

He watched out of the window as she walked

slowly away, then turned back to the matter in hand.

Looking after his own needs—in the form of lunch.

An hour later, he was back on the path, trudging towards a viewpoint where he planned to take another quick break and stare out across at the swell of the ocean while he caught his breath.

There was a long bench sitting proudly on the apex of the clearing, shaded by a fig tree, its branches heavy with fruit. And on that bench, stretched out with her head on her rucksack, was Indigo.

Julien came to a sudden halt and stared at her, his pulse rattling through his veins.

She looked exhausted, her face pink and the exposed part of her neck and upper chest glistening with perspiration in the heat.

His heart gave a jolt at the sight.

He really should keep walking and leave her alone to rest; she hadn't seen him standing there yet, so now would be a good time to turn around and keep on going. He could take a break another half mile or so on.

But he didn't move. Something was stopping him. Some misplaced sense of responsibility.

Sighing, he made his way over to her, resigned to checking that she was okay, thereby clearing his conscience.

She sat up quickly when she noticed him approaching, pulling her rucksack on to her knees and looping her arms around it, as if using it for protection against him.

Did she really have everything she needed for the whole week in that small bag? he wondered fleetingly. His own luggage was about three times the size of hers—hence getting it transported by courier from place to place as he progressed along the walk.

'Hi, Indigo,' he said as he came to a halt in front of her.

Her shoulders stiffened and she gave him a curt nod. 'Julien.'

'How are you today?'

'Fine, thanks. You?' From the tone of her voice she was clearly struggling to be polite.

'Hung-over,' he admitted, giving her a rueful smile.

She didn't smile back.

Tense silence crackled between them, and Indigo's stomach took the opportunity to rumble loudly.

'Have you eaten enough today?' he asked, aiming for an airy, upbeat tone but not quite pulling it off.

She tightened her arms around her bag and gave him a level stare. 'That depends on what you mean by enough.'

'Did you eat lunch?'

There was a pause, where she seemed to be arguing with herself about whether to answer him truthfully. 'No,' she said finally.

'Why not?'

'I wasn't hungry.'

There was an edge to her voice that told him

she wasn't in the mood to be questioned any more about her choices.

'You mean you didn't manage to lift any extra food from the breakfast buffet?' he joked.

Her chin lifted fractionally and her shoulders tensed. 'That's right,' she said with a sarcastic bite to her voice.

It was the dismissive way she deliberately looked away from him into the distance that finally tipped him over the edge. 'You're crazy, you know that? You can't go walking for hours in this heat without eating enough.'

The look she gave him could have frozen water.

Sighing hard, he rummaged in the small rucksack he was carrying his provisions for the walk in and located his emergency energy bar. Striding over to the bench, he held it out towards her.

'Here, take this.'

She looked at the bar with some disdain. 'No, thanks. I don't need anything from you.'

From the tone of her voice, there was undoubtedly a lot more she wanted to add to that statement. Like exactly where he could stick his cereal bar.

Clearly he'd hurt her feelings last night, but, in his defence, he'd been doing her a favour letting her know right away that she was wasting her time if she was expecting anything more to develop between them this week.

Not that he was going to drag that up again right now.

Sighing with impatience, he dropped the energy bar on to the bench next to her, then stepped back, giving her a reproving look.

Okay, he'd done his duty now—he could walk away with integrity.

But, instead of picking up the bar, she stood up and shucked her rucksack on to her back, ignoring it completely.

'Well, it's time I got on with my walk and left you to enjoy the scenery on your *own*. Enjoy the rest of your vacation, Julien,' she said pointedly, echoing his words to her last night.

He watched her walk away from him, his jaw aching with tension as he fought the urge to go after her and tell her to stop being such a stubborn fool and at least stay and rest for a bit longer, the pressure of the denial restarting the throb of pain in his head.

Stomping into Praiano an hour and a half later, with aching legs and a decidedly damp T-shirt sticking to his back, Julien still hadn't shaken the feeling that he should have done more to convince Indigo to take the food he'd offered her.

His failure to persuade her to let him help had reminded him a little too keenly of the struggles he'd had with Celine at the end of their marriage.

Not that the two things could really be compared.

He'd not seen Indigo again on the route; he'd given her a twenty-minute head start after she'd stormed away, which he guessed must mean she'd made it to Praiano without collapsing. At least that was something.

It took him a couple of minutes to locate his hotel, which was in the centre of the small town, and he was about to stride into the glass-fronted lobby when his gaze caught on a familiar figure limping towards him along the pavement to his left.

Indigo didn't appear to notice him standing there and she stopped a few paces away, wrestling her bag off her back and dumping it wearily on to the floor by her feet to pull out her water bottle.

As his gaze followed the movement, he noticed that the trainers she'd chosen to walk for miles and miles in each day were beginning to fall apart, the rubber cracked and peeling away from the material at the sides of the shoe. Surely they couldn't be supporting her feet and ankles properly, and the soles had to be getting thinner and thinner from the rough ground.

Did the woman have *no* sense? Not only was she putting herself in danger of collapse from not eating enough, she was going to end up damaging her feet, or risk skidding off a cliff walking in such unsuitable footwear.

White-hot anger flashed through him at her stupidity, and he stalked towards her, not sure what he was going to say but knowing he needed to say *something* this time.

'Indigo, what are you doing walking in those running shoes over that kind of terrain?' he ground out, frowning hard and jabbing his finger down at her feet.

She took a small step backwards, the alarm on her face at his sudden appearance quickly changing to annoyance.

'What's it to you?' she asked archly, shooting up an eyebrow. 'For someone determined to spend his holiday alone you've got an awful lot to say about the way I spend mine.'

Julien found himself lost for words. She had a point—what was it to him? He wasn't responsible for her and she'd made it perfectly clear she didn't want or need his help.

But someone needed to point out her recklessness to her. Apparently she had no idea how to look after herself.

'Trekking so far in those flimsy shoes is going to damage your feet.'

She took a tiny step towards him. 'I really don't need you to tell me what I should and shouldn't do, thanks very much.'

He matched her step with one of his own. 'You know, I think you're the most stubborn person I've ever met. It seems to me you need someone to point out the obvious or you're going to give yourself a serious injury.'

She let out a large huff of breath, her cheeks flaring with colour. 'Not that it's any of your business, but it wouldn't normally be my choice to go trekking in trainers. If you must know, the airline lost my bag which had my walking boots in it!'

He stared at her, perplexed. 'Why don't you buy yourself some more boots? Surely your insurance will cover it?'

There was a dangerous flash in her eyes. 'Just

go and buy some more boots? With what? I know it's probably hard for someone like you to understand, but some people don't have extra money just lying around in their back pocket. I have nothing in my bank account at the moment and my emergency credit card and half my holiday money also happens to be in my lost bag!'

He could tell from the look in her eyes that she'd reached the end of her tether. Pain and hunger would do that to you.

It suddenly dawned on him what all her previous strange behaviour had been about: the change in hotel after only one night, the stolen lunch, the determination to eat pizza instead of à la carte cuisine.

Money trouble.

'Why haven't you asked your family for help?' he asked, gentling his voice now. 'Surely one of your brothers will lend you some money to tide you over?'

Sighing, she folded her arms and looked down

at her feet, kicking at the ground and wincing. 'Because I don't want to.'

'Why not?'

She looked him directly in the eye again. 'I don't like to rely on other people. I need to know I can survive on my own without any help.'

He gave her a puzzled frown. 'That's impressive. But being able to accept help from others is a skill too.'

She opened her mouth as if to speak, then shut it again, shrugged, then flapped her hand around in an airy manner. 'It's an old habit. It was always do or die in the house where I grew up. Showing any kind of neediness to my brothers was deemed as a sign of weakness.'

This insight into her life disturbed him. 'What about your parents then?'

She paused before she spoke. 'My mum died from breast cancer when I was twelve and my dad passed away a couple of years ago—although, to be honest, he pretty much died when she did, at least his spirit did.'

Her whole posture seemed to shrink in on itself as she folded her arms across her chest. Clearly it was a difficult subject for her to talk about.

'He didn't cope well after she'd gone,' she continued, staring down at the floor, 'so I took over running the household. My brothers certainly didn't have a clue how to do it. Luckily, my mum taught me how to cook before she died and I found I was good at it.' She kicked gently at the ground. 'My dad suffered with bad depression so I ended up staying at home whilst I did my college courses, and then for a few years afterwards.' She shrugged. 'Tough times. But it taught me how to look after myself.'

There was a shadow of sadness in her eyes when she finally looked up at him.

Instinctively, he reached out, giving her arm a sympathetic squeeze. 'I'm sorry.'

'Ah, don't be. I'm okay.'

'That must have been really hard for you.'

She shrugged. 'I survived.'

'No wonder you're so driven.'

Taking a step back, she leant against the wall of the hotel. 'Yeah, well, I wanted to do something good with my life. I wanted to feel like my mum would be proud of me, had she survived. She only made it to forty-four before the cancer killed her. How can that be right? She was a good person. A kind and loving person.'

Her sadness hung thickly in the air between them.

'Some days, life seems anything but fair.'

'Ain't that the truth?'

The haunted look in her eyes broke him.

'Okay, come with me,' he ordered, scooping up her rucksack from the ground and slinging it over his shoulder, then setting off back down the street in the direction she'd come from.

It took a moment for her to come running after him.

'Where are you going with my bag?' she demanded, her breath coming out in short pants after her sprint.

'You'll see.'

'Julien, give it back to me!'

'I will, when we get there.'

'Where?'

'You'll see.'

She growled, low in her throat. 'Now who's being stubborn?'

Luckily, the shop specialising in walking gear that he'd walked past earlier was only another minute's walk away, down the next street, which was a good thing as Indigo was limping hard in her wrecked trainers now.

He ignored her exasperated sigh as he ushered her through the door and into the wonderfully cool air-conditioned interior.

She stopped dead just inside the shop and turned to give him a withering look. 'Julien, I told you, I can't afford to buy new boots right now.'

'I heard you. But you're not buying them. I am.'

Before she could even open her mouth to protest he held up a hand. 'Do not argue with me. I cannot let you walk any more in those monstrosities. It's offending my sensibilities.'

She shook her head. 'Julien, I can't—'

'Quiet, stubborn woman,' he growled in frustration.

Thankfully, she didn't take his tone as an insult, although he was a little perturbed when she burst into laughter instead.

In fact, he started to become seriously worried about her when the laughter seemed to overtake her, bending her double and shaking her whole body as she struggled to get her breathing under control.

When she finally managed to pull herself together, she looked up at him with tears of laughter still in her eyes. 'I'm sorry, I don't know why I'm laughing. I think I'm a bit hysterical. Today has just been a bit *much*, you know? In fact, this whole holiday hasn't exactly turned out the way I expected it to.'

'Yes, this wasn't what I had in mind when I

pictured a break either. I was hoping for a little more peace and quiet and a lot less bickering with pig-headed women,' he said grumpily.

This only made her start laughing again, in great gulping gasps.

All he could do was stand there and wait for her to get a handle on it again.

'I have no idea why the state of my feet troubles you,' she said eventually, taking deep breaths to calm herself down, 'but if it means so much to you then I'll let you buy me some boots.' She swiped the tears from her cheeks and held up a finger. 'But you have to give me your address so I can reimburse you after I get home.'

He shook his head. 'There is no need to pay me back.'

This seemed to sober her up pretty quickly. 'Yes, there is, Julien.'

He could tell from the look on her face that the only way she'd let him help her out was if she felt she could even things out later. Which was fine by him. The cost of the boots meant nothing to him, but he knew this wasn't really about the money. It was about pride.

'Okay. Agreed,' he said, giving her a resigned smile. Catching the sales assistant's eye, he waved for her to come over.

'Now, let's get you sorted out.'

CHAPTER FIVE

Discovering Praiano—a simple town with a big heart. Check out the small pebbled cove, which is especially atmospheric in the evening...

THE NEW BOOTS felt wonderful on her feet.

Despite her protests, Julien had insisted on buying her some specialised walking socks and plasters too, in an attempt to protect her poor blistered skin from more damage. She was now wearing all the things they'd purchased and had dropped her ruined trainers into the shop's recycling bin with a huge sigh of relief.

The day was finally starting to look up.

After finally arriving in Praiano, footsore, disgruntled and almost faint with hunger, she'd hit rock bottom when she'd arrived at her hotel to find her bag still hadn't turned up.

She'd nearly cried, right there at the reception desk.

In fact, she was just on her way to grab the cheapest, most calorific meal she could find in the town centre to try and boost her morale when Julien had shown up out of the blue and marched her over to the hiking store.

Even though she felt hugely uncomfortable about him spending money on her, at that precise moment she hadn't had the strength to put up more of a fight.

That was why she'd given in so easily.

That and the fact she'd been acutely aware of something in his eyes when he'd argued with her—something that made her think he'd needed to win this small battle. Maybe it was just a macho male impulse to assert his authority, but for some reason she didn't believe that was the whole of it. Even though he'd made it clear he didn't want anything more to do with her, he hadn't been able to turn a blind eye when he'd seen how she was struggling.

Just the fact he'd noticed that she was in trouble made her feel like she wanted to cry again, only this time with gratitude. It felt like a long time since someone had looked out for her like that.

Argh! And now she was starting to like him again, when she'd told herself to stay well out of his way.

After exiting the shop with Julien hot on her newly shod heels, they stood awkwardly on the pavement, looking anywhere but at each other. She expected him to make some excuse any second now to get away from the strange tension deadening the air between them, but he didn't move, instead turning to look at her with that perplexed frown of his.

'Why don't you go for a short walk in your boots, to check they're fitting properly?' he said, breaking eye contact to glance down at her feet. 'Just in case you need to take them back. I'm guessing you're walking on to Positano tomorrow, so you won't have an opportunity to swap them after today.'

'Yes, I am,' she said. 'That's a good idea.' Swinging her bag on to her back, she took a pace backwards. 'What are you going to do?' she asked, trying to make the question sound as casual as possible. What was the etiquette here? Should she invite him to come along? It felt rude to just stride off when he'd gone to the trouble of helping her out. But, then again, would she be putting him in an awkward position where he'd feel forced to reject her again?

'Why don't I come with you?' he said, surprising her. 'The assistant didn't seem to know much English and you might need me to translate again.' He frowned and shook his head. 'At least I'm assuming you don't speak Italian? I never asked.'

'You assume correctly.' It had pleased her to find out she'd been right about his linguistic skills. When the sales assistant had come over and they'd started speaking to her in English and she'd not understood the nuances of what they wanted, Julien had switched to Italian. To her untrained ear it sounded as flawless as his English. Which proved her theory that he'd been speaking her language for her benefit the night they'd shared the honeymoon suite. Something about this discovery gave her a little lift of joy.

'I can order a coffee and ask where the bathrooms are, but that's about the extent of my vocabulary without consulting a phrase book,' she said with a smile.

'*Bon*. I'll come with you then.'

'Don't you want to check into your hotel?'

He shook his head. 'Later.'

'Okay,' she said, shrugging, trying not to give away how pleased she was that he wasn't just going to abandon her now. 'I'm going to grab a sandwich from that shop over there before I die of hunger, but I can eat it while we walk.'

'We can sit down. I'm not in a rush.'

'Are you sure?'

'Yes. Sure.'

So, she bought a panini stuffed with prosciutto and nutty-tasting cheese and the sweetest sun-dried tomatoes she'd even eaten and sat at a long counter in the shop and consumed the whole thing in about two minutes flat. Julien stood next to her, drinking an espresso, not saying a word about her eating habits, though she could practically hear him thinking the words, *See? You were a fool not to take that energy bar when I offered it to you.*

Maybe she had been a little foolish, but she'd still been angry with him at the time for the way he'd spoken to her the night before, and had chosen her pride over her stomach.

After that they wandered out of the town centre and away towards the cliffs, enjoying the cool breeze coming off the sea. It was still hot, but much more bearable now that the sun had begun to slip down behind the horizon.

'Let's go and check out the beach,' she suggested, fully expecting him to say no and make his excuses to leave now.

He paused for a moment, his expression unreadable, before nodding slowly. 'Sure,' he said, surprising her again with the warmth in his voice.

They made their way over to where a winding set of steps led down to the small pebbled beach. The sharp, briny smell of the sea hit her nose as they picked their way across to the centre of the deserted cove, the only sound coming from the rush of waves and the melodic tinkle of the stones as the water played back and forth over them.

She stopped near the water's edge and looked out towards the horizon, where the sun was disappearing from view, leaving the soft glow of dusk in its wake.

'Wow. It really is beautiful here,' she said as Julien came to a halt beside her.

They stood side by side and stared out at the gentle swell of the water in silence, listening to the faraway cries of the birds wheeling in the sky above them.

When she turned to glance at Julien, she was surprised to find he was looking at her with a strange little pinch between his brows.

A wave of tingling warmth washed from head to foot, pooling deep inside her as their gazes locked. She knew it was ridiculous to read anything into it, but something felt different between them now, as if a layer of armour had been peeled away.

Clearing her throat, she tore her gaze away and rummaged in her bag, desperate for something to distract her from the fizz of nerves in her tummy, producing her book on walking the Amalfi coast and her eyeliner. 'Here,' she said, thrusting them towards him. 'Write your address inside the front cover, will you? Then I'll know where to send the money.'

Without a word, he took them from her and, twitching his eyebrows at her choice of writing implement, wrote in the book.

She watched him move his strong, blunt-tipped fingers across the page, marvelling at how elegant his writing was.

He was a man of such contradictions.

'Why did you do this for me?' she blurted, unable to keep her speculation to herself any longer.

He glanced up at her, his eyes narrowing in thought. 'I don't like to see anyone in trouble, especially when I can do something to fix the problem easily.'

His choice of the word 'anyone' made her stomach drop a little with disappointment. 'You mean by throwing money at it?' she said, perhaps a little too snippily.

He raised an eyebrow. 'If that's what it takes.'

How lucky to have that luxury, she thought. But she didn't say it out loud. It would only have sounded petty and churlish.

'Well, thank you.' She took the book and eyeliner back from him and slid them carefully back into her bag.

There was an uncomfortable pause where they stood looking at each other again.

Indigo was aware of her heart beating hard against her ribcage as she tried to make sense of what was going on here. Why was he still here talking to her? Was it because he felt sorry for her? She hoped that wasn't it.

'Look, Indigo, I should apologise for being so rude last night at dinner.'

She couldn't meet his gaze, the memory of the humiliation she'd felt burning through her once again. 'Forget about it. It doesn't matter.'

'Yes, it does.' He moved his head to the side, then bent towards her, waiting until he'd caught her eye before he spoke again. 'Indigo, it does. I'm not normally so unfriendly; you've just caught me at a bad time.'

She gave him a shaky smile, cocking her head and splaying out her hands on either side of her. 'Okay, I accept your apology.'

There was relief in his eyes and something else.

Her lips tingled as his gaze dropped to her mouth and her pulse rocketed.

He looked like—

—he wanted to—

—*kiss* her.

The thought lit a fire inside her, burning through her veins and turning her nerve endings into a crackling mass of need.

Ever since she'd laid eyes on him she'd wondered what it would feel like to have those strong arms wrapped around her, holding her close, comforting and sheltering her. And those wide, firm lips pressed against hers, smoothing away her loneliness.

The air felt thick with longing as his eyes met hers again. They seemed to darken as she parted her lips to drag warm, salty air deep into her lungs in an attempt to calm her erratic heartbeat.

Something seemed to be pulling her towards him, some strange magnetic instinct, and she took a microstep forwards to maintain her balance, raising her hand to his face.

He let out a low, rough breath as her fingers connected with the lightly stubbled skin of his jaw, and then suddenly Julien was no longer there in front of her, but far, far away.

Too far.

'What—?' She blinked in shock, stumbling forwards, dazed by the sudden desertion.

He was standing a few paces back from her now, shaking his head, his eyes a little wild. He held up a hand, his face a picture of remorse. 'That's not what I'm here for, Indigo.' He shook his head, his expression heavy with regret and frustration. 'I'm in no position to—' He waved a hand in her direction, his movements jerky and agitated.

'To what?'

'Do this.'

'I don't even know what *this* is, Julien.'

He took another step away from her and

rubbed a hand across his face. 'I need my freedom right now, Indigo. I need to be alone.'

She snorted in angry frustration, every inch of her skin feeling hot and prickly. 'It was just going to be a kiss. A bit of fun. It didn't have to mean anything.'

If only that were true. Perhaps if it were then her voice wouldn't sound as if she'd just been picked up and shaken hard.

He screwed up his face in frustration. 'It's never just a bit of fun though, is it?' There was a look of admonishment in his eyes that made her stomach drop to the floor.

How embarrassing. She'd read the situation all wrong—though, to be fair to her, she hadn't come here looking for romance. She was just going with the flow, enjoying the adventure, seeing where the day took her.

Not that she hadn't considered the possibility of something more developing between them after he'd agreed to come down here with her. His change in mood had made her wonder whether there could be something more to this.

Something exciting. Something good.

But clearly she was wrong.

'What is it you're afraid of, Julien?' she asked, her tone a little defensive as she fought to maintain her pride.

He took another step away from her, rubbing a hand through his hair, messing up the neat waves. He looked back at her with such exasperation on his face it made her want to move towards him and smooth it away.

Which, of course, she couldn't.

Instead, she tried to smile as if it all meant nothing to her, which proved impossible because it felt as though the corners of her mouth were being dragged down by some kind of extreme gravitational force. 'I'm sorry. I didn't mean to pry.'

He looked at her for the longest time, his troubled gaze searching her face as if he wanted to say more but couldn't find the right words. Finally, he held up his hand, as if putting up a barrier between them. 'I'm going to go,' he said, taking a step away from her, his posture dipping a little as the pebbles gave way under his feet. 'It's for the best.'

And then he turned, his shoulders tense and his hands clenched into fists, and strode away from her until he disappeared into the inky-dark night.

CHAPTER SIX

Praiano to Positano—traversing the Path of the Gods. Be aware, this part of the walk includes vertiginous sections with breath-taking views...

JULIEN DIDN'T SLEEP well again.

Only this time his dreams weren't tangled with thoughts of his ex-wife and his failed marriage. Instead, they kept coming back to the intensity of the moment he'd shared with Indigo on the beach. Over and over again, as if the memory was stuck on repeat.

In his half wakeful state the next morning, he relived the overpowering instinct he'd felt to hold her close, to experience the strength of her wrapped around him, to taste her sweetness—only then to feel the wrench of guilt for almost indulging his cravings when he had no intention of following through on his physical promises.

There was no wonder she'd looked so wounded when he'd pushed her away. He'd practically accused her of being the one to lead their strange, lustful dance.

He'd been just as much to blame. More so, probably.

He'd wanted her.

But he had no right to indulge his wants. Not in the mindset he was in at the moment.

He'd known at the time that he was going too far—way too far—when he'd agreed to go down to the beach with her, but despite the warnings flashing through his mind, he'd not been able to walk away and leave her.

He'd been greedy for more time with Indigo Hughes.

It had felt so good to be able to take charge of her challenging situation and do something to help. After the sheer frustration of failing to save his marriage, it had fortified something inside him—given him the satisfaction that he hadn't lost his ability to take care of people when they needed help. Even if it had been for a near enough stranger.

Not that Indigo felt like a stranger to him any more. After hearing about how she'd lost both her parents and her struggles growing up in such a tough emotional environment, she'd become vividly real to him now. Which, of course, was part of the problem.

Standing on that beach in the quiet of dusk, watching the day change into another dark, solitary night, he'd wanted her to know what an incredible, impressive and attractive person he thought she was. At that moment making a connection with her had seemed important for some reason.

But, in doing so, he'd nearly stepped over the line and once again proved just how selfish he could be.

Giving up on getting any more sleep, he decided to set off early from the hotel in order to miss most of the other walkers on his way to Positano.

A couple of hours into the walk, he'd been enjoying getting into the soothing rhythm of it, letting his mind wander freely, when he found himself on a particularly narrow part of the path which began to swing gradually out closer to the cliff's edge. It was only when he dragged himself out of his philosophical thoughts to take proper stock of what he was heading for that he realised the next part of the walk was going to take him past some unguarded sections where the exposed cliff edge fell steeply away from the path, straight down to the rocks below.

A bead of sweat trickled down his spine, followed swiftly by another as he carefully continued on the path, which, to his growing unease, was becoming narrower and narrower the further along it he walked.

He'd never been great with heights, but he'd never before experienced this dizzying horror as he took in the sight of the sea crashing against razor-sharp rocks below him. If only there had been a railing he could touch, to reassure himself there was no way he could stumble and fall down into what seemed in his unsettled imaginings to be oblivion.

His breath came fast now, scything in and out of his lungs and burning his parched throat as his pace slowed to a crawl. A gravitational force seemed to be pulling at him, attempting to draw him closer and closer to the edge as he picked his way along the path. Looking behind him, he wondered wildly for a moment whether he should go back, but the thought of even turning around on the narrow path caused a wave of pure terror to flood through his body and his stomach to lurch, bringing him to the edge of nausea.

It would be so easy to topple to the side and fall. He could picture the air rushing past him, feel the impending doom as he rocketed closer and closer to the jagged rocks, then the unforgiving suck of the sea as it pulled him into its fathomless depths.

His heart was pounding so hard he could feel it in his throat.

Closing his eyes, he grabbed for the foliage that rose to the right of him to steady himself and somehow managed to anchor himself enough to slide down on to his haunches with his back to the rough stone wall, pressing himself hard against it.

The solid feel of rock and earth steadied him and he opened his eyelids a crack to take stock of his situation.

Not good.

He was roughly halfway along the dangerously narrow path, with no easy way forward or back.

He was stuck.

Why the heck hadn't he bought himself a walking guidebook, like the last hotel receptionist had suggested? If he had, he'd have known what he was about to face and could either have taken a longer inland route or skipped this section of the walk completely and taken a bus to the next destination.

But then that hadn't been the point of the trip. He was here to challenge his endurance and push through any personal discomfort until he felt like himself again. Skipping part of it would have felt like cheating on the promise he'd made to himself.

But what a challenge it had turned out to be.

Adrenaline had raised his blood pressure, heating his body as he fought the flight impulse so that he felt as though he was sitting in an oven—the fierce heat of the sun beating down on his head was not helping his cause.

What felt like an age later, the sound of voices floated towards him from the direction he'd come, and he turned his head to see who it was, humiliation already engulfing him at the thought of what he would look like, hunched over, clinging on to the rock face.

Pretty unheroic, he suspected.

A minute later a group of men that he'd not encountered before walked up to him on the path, all of them giving him an odd look as they picked their way carefully past him.

'Buongiorno,' he muttered to them, raising his head and forcing a friendly smile on to his face.

'Everything okay?' one of them asked in Italian as he passed, his brow crinkled with concern.

'Great, fine,' Julien muttered, flapping a hand in the air. 'Just taking a quick break,' he added, quickly lowering his hand again to grip back on to the rocky surface.

The man's frown deepened, but he didn't stop walking, giving a shrug and picking up his pace to catch up with his friends.

Letting out a low sigh, Julien pressed his head back against the wall again and tried to think himself out of his problem. This was ridiculous; he was a grown man of thirty-six, he should not be letting a bit of rock and air defeat him.

Blowing gently first up towards his forehead, then down towards his chest, he attempted to think cooling thoughts to regulate his heartbeat, then, when that didn't work, he tried distracting himself by thinking about work. But his mind kept leaping back to how close he was to the edge, which made him laugh out loud in a maniacal fashion because it occurred to him then that his whole world seemed to be full of edges that he was trying not to fall off at the moment.

Which inevitably made him think about Indigo. He shifted uncomfortably on his haunches as he thought again about the look of hurt in those beautiful eyes of hers—the look he'd caused—and he nearly toppled forwards.

That woman would be the death of him. Literally.

Another age passed while he tried to gather himself enough to stand up and force himself to walk along the rest of the path. It couldn't be that much further until it wound back inland. Could it?

Just as he was about to attempt to heave himself back to standing, the sound of more voices coming towards him made him freeze in dismay.

Taking a deep breath and cursing himself for picking such a popular walking route to be stranded on, he steeled himself to make polite conversation again until they'd gone. He really didn't want to have any witnesses to his humiliation, so he was going to wave them on and wait until they were well out of sight before he made his next attempt at getting off this damn cliff.

He readied himself, fixing a smile firmly on to his face and was about to turn towards the approaching group when he realised with a lurch that he recognised one of the voices.

Oh, no. Please, no. Anyone but her.

After counting to three, which did absolutely nothing to calm his raging pulse, he turned his head to watch Indigo walk towards him, followed by three women he didn't recognise.

His heart sank. Was this karma coming along to kick his butt? Or, since this was Indigo we were talking about—fate?

Her brow creased into a frown as she got nearer to where he was sitting, which wasn't entirely unjustified since he was taking up half of the path so that anyone wanting to journey on would have to step around him, putting themselves in even more danger of slipping off the edge of the cliff and into the sea.

'Julien, are you okay?' Indigo asked, her voice edged with unease. That would be due to the insulting I-want-you-no-I-don't debacle he'd put her through last night.

'I'm fine, Indigo,' he managed to rasp through a throat that had practically closed up with embarrassment.

Her frown deepened, but she kept on walking, stepping past him so that the women close on her heels could get by too.

Thankfully, none of the others spoke to him and he averted his gaze, willing away the raging heat in his face as he counted down the seconds until they'd be out of his sight line and he could make another attempt at standing up and leaving this godforsaken place.

There was a murmur of voices in the distance,

which he assumed was Indigo filling the rest of her party in on the tribulations he'd put her through since they'd first clapped eyes on each other, and he dropped his head to his knees and let out a long, low breath.

So this was what payback felt like.

Indigo made it a few more metres down the path—after breezily explaining to the three women she'd made friends with at breakfast that Julien was just another hiker she'd met on the walk—when her conscience refused to let her take another step.

There had been something odd in Julien's expression when she'd walked up to him that had lodged itself in her head, and she couldn't shake the feeling that something had been very wrong, despite his assertions to the contrary.

After the humiliating episode last night she'd been determined to forget about him now and carry on with her holiday in the way she'd planned. She'd be coolly friendly, of course if—

no, *when*—they bumped into each other again, but that would be it.

She wasn't going to put herself in a position where she made a fool of herself in front of him again. Because she didn't need an emotional roller-coaster ride like that right now.

She was supposed to be looking after herself this week.

But something about the way he was sitting there still niggled at her.

'I'm going to go back and check that Julien's okay,' she told her new friends, experiencing a dip of disappointment at leaving them when they'd all been getting on so well.

'Okay. Perhaps we'll see you in Positano,' the more senior of the women, Ruth, said, giving her a friendly smile. There was something else in her expression too, as if she suspected there was a little more to Indigo's about-turn than she was admitting to.

Not that it mattered what Ruth thought. Julien had helped her out by getting her the boots she was currently wearing, thus saving her holiday, and she owed him big for that.

He was probably fine anyway and would wave her concerns away in that arrogant way of his, so she'd be able to catch her new friends up again— but she just wanted to make sure.

Julien looked as though he was about to stand up as she made her way back to him along the rough, narrow path. She began to feel foolish for worrying and was about to turn round again when she noticed that the tendons in his hands were white with tension as he clung to the rock behind him, and a sheen of perspiration had broken out across his forehead.

What was going on here? Was he ill?

'Julien? Are you sure you're okay?' she asked as she came within striking distance of him.

He dropped his chin to his chest at the sound of her voice, as if he was exasperated with her for coming back and bothering him.

A sting of annoyance jabbed her, but she didn't back off. 'Are you feeling ill?'

He lifted his head to look at her and she could tell by the expression on his face that her instincts had been right. There was something badly wrong here.

There was a long pause where she worried whether he was even capable of answering her. Then she saw him swallow hard before letting out a long, frustrated sigh.

'I was fine with the first bit of this walk,' he said, his voice sounding strained, 'but then the path got narrower and I started to feel like the ground was sloping downwards towards the drop, which made me dizzy. Logically, I know it isn't doing that, but my brain keeps telling me otherwise. I've never been great with heights, but I haven't been affected this badly before.'

He was afraid of heights? No wonder he looked so distressed.

'Didn't you read about this bit in your guidebook?' she asked, wondering how the heck she was going to help him get out of here. It wasn't as if she could toss him over her shoulder and carry him the rest of the way.

He let out a huff of breath. 'What guidebook?'

'You don't have a guidebook with you?'

'*Non*. I'm—what do you English say?—*winging it*. I wanted to experience this holiday without any expectations.'

She couldn't help but laugh at the superior expression on his face. 'You are the most mercurial man I've ever met,' she said, unable to stop herself from teasing him. After the way he'd acted last night it was somewhat satisfying to get one over on him.

He gave her a rueful grin. 'I'm glad I amuse you.'

She could tell from the shake in his voice that he was genuinely rattled, though. It must be a terrifying thing, believing that you're stuck alone on the side of a cliff face, not able to go either forwards or back the way you came.

That thought galvanised her.

'Okay, this is what we're going to do. You're

going to walk on the inside with one hand touching the wall or foliage and I'll walk next to you on the open side. You look ahead, but slightly inland so you're not looking at the drop the whole way along. I'll make sure we stay safely on the path. Okay?'

He stared at her for a moment, then blinked as if her words had taken a moment to sink in. 'Are you sure you want to do that?'

Once again she realised there was much more to his question than its face value. She knew what he was really asking.

Shaking her head, she put her hands on her hips. 'You think just because we had a minor disagreement I'm going to walk away and leave you here?'

His mouth twitched at the corner and he shook his head. 'No. That doesn't seem like the sort of thing you'd do.' He sighed, his exasperation with himself clear. 'Okay. Let's do it.'

'Okay then. Now, give me your hand.'

He looked up at her and frowned. 'What?'

'Don't worry, I'm not trying to seduce you,' she said, laying on the sarcasm. 'It will keep you grounded.'

'What if I fall and pull you over with me? I don't want to be responsible for tipping us both off a cliff.'

She let out a huff of breath at the doubt in his voice, but reined her irritation back in. 'That's not going to happen; I have fantastic balance. Now, give me your hand.'

Taking a breath, he let go of the rocks behind him and lifted his hand tentatively towards her.

She grasped it in one of hers. 'Okay, good. Now stand up slowly.'

He did so, wobbling a little as he righted himself and faced the direction in which they needed to go.

'Great, we're set,' she said, feeling the tension in his grip. 'Just keep looking at the wall and I'll guide us safely forwards.'

They set off slowly, Julien's steps hesitant at first, but becoming more sure as they made their way slowly along the pathway. Their clasped hands grew sweaty in the heat, but she didn't let go of him to wipe them on her shorts. She didn't think he'd appreciate that.

'Talk to me, take my mind off that thousand-metre drop just inches away,' he said when he wobbled a little at one point.

'I think a thousand metres might be a slight exaggeration—'

'It doesn't feel like it to me,' he cut in gruffly.

She bit back a smile. 'What do you want to talk about?'

'Anything. I don't care. Tell me about the people that you're teaching to cook.'

'Oh, my goodness… Well, there are some real characters in my cooking group.'

'I can imagine.'

'There's one guy whose wife left him six months ago after forty years of marriage because she was fed up with him being so insensitive and lazy. He's learning how to cook so he can woo her back.'

'Is it working?'

'It seems so.' She grinned at the memory. 'Apparently his spaghetti *sorry, babe* was a real hit and she's going back this week to sample his apple *turnover a new leaf.*'

She continued to tell him anecdotes about the people she'd come into contact with in the last year, actually starting to enjoy herself as she remembered things she'd not thought about for a while. It reminded her of how rewarding it had felt to make a difference in these people's lives. Even if it was only in some small way.

Julien listened intently, chiming in every now and again with a gruff question or comment, and by the time they reached the end of the vertiginous section and had come out into a wider, flatter path, his voice sounded almost normal again.

She was glad to have been able to help him, even though, as usual, he'd made it unnecessarily difficult for her.

The man was too proud for his own good—

but she wasn't going to hold it against him. She knew all about pride.

It occurred to her that if she'd been here with Gavin and it had been her that had been scared of heights he would have lorded that weakness over her—even though he would have disguised it as teasing—and he wouldn't have let her forget about it for the rest of the holiday.

There was no way she was going to do that to Julien, and she felt sure he wouldn't have done it to her if the roles were reversed; he seemed too classy for that.

She awkwardly extricated her hand from his vice-like grip, somewhat disappointed now to let go. It had been nice having that connection with him as they'd talked.

He seemed a little surprised by the loss of her touch and turned to look at her with his brow drawn into a frown.

'Are you okay now?' she asked.

'Yes, I'm fine. My heart doesn't feel like it's going to explode in my chest any more.'

He looked away towards where the azure-blue ocean crashed noisily against the rocks far below them.

She gazed at his profile, taking in the strength of his jaw with its faint show of bristles, noting a small scar where the bone swooped up towards his ear. She wondered briefly how he'd got it, then pushed away the instinct to ask him. It was probably too personal a question and he might get snippy about answering it.

To be honest, she was a little hurt that he wasn't being friendlier to her after she'd just rescued him from certain doom. Not that she'd done it to be lavished with gratitude and praise, but to hear a simple thank you wouldn't hurt. Perhaps his alpha pride had been dented and this was his way of shutting the humiliation of it out.

But, even so—

He turned back suddenly, making her jump a little as the shock of the movement yanked her out of her reverie.

Taking a pace backwards, he folded his arms tightly against his chest.

She tried not to notice how this made the sculpted muscles in his arms bulge in a rather attractive way.

'So you should consider your debt for the boots paid off,' he bit out, his face dark with a frown.

Great. An acknowledgement. Sort of. It wasn't exactly a heartfelt outpouring of thanks, though.

'You do know there are more sheer drops on the next leg of the walk, don't you?' Indigo blurted with a reproachful lift of her eyebrow, unable to keep her annoyance at him spilling over.

His face seemed to pale. 'Really?'

'You know, I'd be happy to partner with you for that bit if you like,' she said loftily, 'just in case you need me to distract you with my witty repartee till we get past them.'

As soon as she'd said the words she regretted them. Not because she didn't want to spend more time with him, but because she knew, deep down, that it wasn't altruism that had prompted her to make the offer; it was because she enjoyed being around him. Even though there was a good chance she was letting herself in for more hurt and rejection here, she couldn't quite tear herself away from him just yet.

He captivated her with his strange mixture of gruff pride and compassion, not to mention the way he made her tummy flip when he looked at her with his impassioned, penetrating gaze.

She wondered again what could have happened to his marriage to make him so defensive.

'Why would you want to do that?' he asked brusquely.

'Because I'm the better person,' she joked, flashing him a grin, which he countered with a raised eyebrow.

She threw up her hands in exasperation. 'Okay, how about we say each day of walking pays off a boot? In my mind, that makes us even.'

'Okay,' he shot back. 'Fine.' He followed the word with a long, agitated sigh and glanced down once more at the sea beneath them. 'Now, let's put some more distance between us and this death trap and get to Positano before nightfall.'

They didn't speak again until they reached the outskirts of the town and checked the details of their lodgings for the night, which suited Julien just fine. After the humiliation of finding himself at such a disadvantage and having to rely on Indigo's goodwill to get him out of trouble, he'd just wanted to sink into his own head for a while.

Not that he hadn't been intensely aware of her presence beside him the whole way there. He'd been impressed with her fitness levels too—she'd not asked to stop once, even after a particularly steep ascent. No wonder she was in such good shape.

He forced the tantalising image of her lean, fit body that followed that thought right out of his head.

'We're staying on the same road,' Indigo said,

throwing him an *it must be fate* smile. 'But I'm a bit further down the hill.'

'Bon,' he replied, desperate for some solitude now so he could get a handle on these frustratingly conflicting feelings she'd stirred up in him.

He was intensely aware that in another life he would have jumped at the chance to make more of their connection—but that he couldn't act on his impulses, not here, not now. It wouldn't be fair to either of them. Despite the whispered demands of his body, his mind kept reminding him he couldn't offer her any kind of emotional commitment.

And from what he already knew of her, he could tell that wouldn't work for Indigo.

But the thought of saying goodbye to her now also twisted something inside him.

They reached the road they needed barely a minute later.

'Well, this is me,' she said, nodding towards the place where she was going to bed down for the night, with its simple crazy-paved stone frontage and garish sign that shouted: *cheap, but cheerful!*

'And that's me,' he said with a nod towards a much grander building sitting proudly a little further up the hill, with clear sea views and an elegant iron-railed terrace for every room.

Only a little further up the road, but worlds apart.

'Indigo—'

'Yes?'

'Thank you for not abandoning me to my fate today.'

He felt like a fool for saying it, but her expression lightened as if she was relieved to finally hear it.

His acknowledgement didn't stop her from winding him up, though.

'That wasn't fate trying to tip you off a cliff, it was just reminding you that you should be nicer to me.'

He rubbed a hand over his face and snorted. She was right, of course; he hadn't exactly been chivalrous about accepting her help. He'd been so embarrassed his manners seemed to have fled him.

'Okay, point taken.' Despite being desperate for some time alone, he knew he should at least attempt to show some appreciation for what she'd done for him today. She'd certainly gone above and beyond the call of duty. 'Can I buy you dinner tonight? To show my gratitude.'

She shifted on her feet, looking uncomfortable. 'You don't need to do that. I think we're even with the boots.'

She wouldn't meet his eye and her body language made him think about how she'd looked on the beach after they'd been so close—so dangerously close—to kissing. The sensory memory was so acute he could have sworn he caught the same briny scent on the air mixed with her sweet floral fragrance.

He shook it off and folded his arms. 'Look, Indigo, what happened last night on the beach—I never meant to lead you into thinking I was interested in a holiday fling. The truth is, I'm not in a good place right now. I've only just signed my divorce papers and, to be honest, I can't see myself wanting another relationship any time soon.'

She looked at him sharply, her brow pinched, and held up a hand. 'It's okay, Julien, I'm not interested in a fling either. I just came here for a break. To walk and see the magnificent scenery. That's all.'

He looked into her wide grey eyes and saw only steady resolve there. 'Okay then.' He cleared his throat, which felt strangely wadded and tight. 'Well, let's meet here at eight o'clock tomorrow,' he said. 'We should bring enough food to see us through to Nerano. Or, if you prefer, I can ask the receptionist where we can find a place to stop for lunch?'

She grinned at his rather clipped tone and rolled her eyes at him. 'Don't worry, I'll bring a packed lunch with me so you won't need to carry me past the finishing line.'

'Good,' he said, with one chastising eyebrow raised.

'Good,' she replied, pressing her lips into a pugnacious smile.

There was a voice in the back of his head warning him again about the wisdom of getting too friendly with her, but he pushed it aside. Neither of them were stupid; they knew what this was.

But, more importantly, they knew now what it wasn't.

CHAPTER SEVEN

Positano to Nerano via Sant'Agata. More vertiginous drops with a ridgetop walk and views for miles. Going for a reinvigorating swim in the ocean is a must at the end of this hard day's walk...

So, WALKING PARTNERS it was.

At least that would mean they could stop trying to avoid each other at every turn when it was clear they were destined to walk this path together, both metaphorically and physically, Indigo mused as she finished her breakfast the next morning.

She'd been really tempted to take him up on his offer of dinner last night, so much so that she'd had a physical pain in the back of her throat as she forced out her refusal, but she knew she had to be sensible here. There could be a danger she was reverting to type and turning him into a project, thinking she could help or even fix him without getting hurt—just like she had with Gavin—and that wasn't something she wanted to put herself through again.

Ugh! Was it going to be like this every time she met someone she was attracted to? Damn Gavin and his ability to make her feel so paranoid. So she liked helping people! What was so wrong with that?

Still, even if Julien had been willing to embark on a holiday fling with her, giving in to her attraction was a definite no-no. She'd be a fool to get entangled with him when he was so emotionally unavailable and she was still feeling sore after being given the boot by Gavin.

This holiday was supposed to be about looking after *her* for a change, she reminded herself for what felt like the millionth time.

After making sure she'd packed everything into her small rucksack, all the while giving herself a stern talking-to about keeping her fascination with him under wraps today, she checked out and left the hotel to meet Julien.

He was waiting for her where they'd agreed to meet the night before, looking just as perfectly turned out as usual, though his eyes were ringed with dark circles and he clearly hadn't bothered to shave. The sight of Julien with rough edges gave her a delicious little shiver of pleasure, which she quickly stamped on before it got the better of her.

Sighing, she tugged hard on her backpack straps to tighten them.

It was going to be a long day.

After a slightly awkward greeting they strode away from Positano, both a little quiet to begin with, but after a few false starts at conversation they fell into a comfortable rhythm, finding a surprisingly diverse array of subjects to chat about, including a somewhat heated discussion about whether London or Paris was the better city to live in.

'But we have amazing markets in London! Like Spitalfields and Notting Hill and the Columbia Road Flower Market,' Indigo interjected when Julien suggested that Paris was the best city in the world for street markets.

'Well, we have the best architecture,' he countered.

'London is full of great buildings, including lots of new ones,' she pointed out. 'The Shard, for example. It's way taller and more impressive than any of the buildings in Paris. Parisians seem to be totally averse to moving with the times and building anything new.'

'Ah, but we have the Eiffel Tower, which beats The Shard hands down for style,' he threw back, as if that answered everything. 'And I would hate to live in a place that was a perpetual building site.'

In fact, they were so engrossed in their back and forth banter about which city ruled supreme that Julien barely seemed to notice when she slid her hand into his as they reached the spot where one side of the path fell away to a sheer drop, as if it was the most natural thing in the world for her to do.

She thought he seemed a little less tense than he'd been the day before as they traversed the exposed section, moving their conversation on to debate the pros and cons of being part of the Euro. He seemed so engrossed, in fact, that Indigo found herself enjoying a sense of achievement at managing to distract him enough for his vertigo to not have been too much of a problem today.

Then later, chatting over lunch, it turned out they were both big fans of psychological suspense and they got into another animated discussion comparing the top writers of the genre, which took till they reached the fortress-like outskirts of Sant'Agata to conclude.

It had been so wonderful to talk about things they both felt passionate about that Indigo arrived in the town having really enjoyed her walk today.

Her hotel for the night was located on the out-skirts, to the east of the town, which meant they walked straight past it once they'd left the trail.

'I'm going to use their bathroom to splash some water on my face before I leave you,' Julien said, following her up to the entrance and into the wonderfully cool interior.

'Okay,' Indigo replied, watching him stride away, feeling a mixture of apprehension and regret as she made her way to the reception desk.

Her insides felt twisted. Would this be the last they'd see of each other now that the more perilous parts of the walk were over? She couldn't imagine Julien wanting to continue holiday-ing with her now that she wasn't needed, not after what he'd told her about wanting time on his own to get his head together. Her stomach clenched with dismay. She'd so enjoyed getting to know him better today and had been surprised and excited by how much their tastes and beliefs had aligned.

They seemed to be kindred spirits.

Had he felt it too?

'Indigo Hughes—I have a reservation here for tonight,' she said absently to the receptionist when he looked up to greet her, her head still full of thoughts about Julien disappearing from her life now. She knew he'd think it was foolish, but she'd begun to wonder whether they'd been thrown together here for a reason. Ever since she'd met him she'd been filled with an unexpected buzz of hope and excitement for the future, which had been sadly lacking in her personal life for some time.

'Ah, yes, Signorina Hughes, I have a bag for you here,' the receptionist said.

She stared at him, her brain taking a while to switch gears and take in what he'd just said to her.

'Did you say you've got my bag? From the airport?' she asked, her voice trembling with excitement.

'*Si,*' the receptionist said, leaving the desk to

go into a small room behind reception and returning with her rucksack.

Indigo nearly fell to her knees with relief. After surviving with virtually nothing for half her holiday, it was absolute bliss to have her possessions returned to her. She took the large rucksack from his outstretched hands and hugged it to her like a lost child, then dropped it on to a nearby sofa in the lobby and yanked open the drawstring to check everything was still in there.

Julien returned from the bathroom to find her in a state of ecstasy as she rummaged through the bag, having pulled out first her money, then her phone and now her bikini.

'I can finally go for a swim! I've been desperate to get into the sea but I didn't want to scare the other holidaymakers by stripping down to my sensibly supportive but utterly hideous underwear,' she said, grinning at him.

He stood watching her with an amused smile as she continued to pull things out of her bag and hug them to her.

It felt a little like her birthday and Christmas had all come at once.

Except for the rather unsettling fact that she was about to say goodbye to Julien, of course. It seemed like such a shame when they'd just started getting on so well. Though there was always the possibility they might bump into each other again on the route.

'So, I guess you should be okay with the rest of the walk from this point on,' she said, forcing her mouth into a cheery smile. 'I don't think there are any more exposed paths to worry about.'

Crossing his arms, he leant his hip against the backrest of the sofa. 'Actually, I'm hiring a boat from Nerano. I'm going to sail north along the coast and stop off at some of the places of interest along the way.'

The hope she'd not wanted to fully acknowledge vanished in a puff of smoke and was replaced by a heavy thump of disappointment. So this really was it then. There would be no more opportunities to bump into him. She'd so enjoyed getting to know him today. It had been the most fun day she'd had since she got here. She'd loved the way he challenged and argued with her. Gavin had never stood up to her like that; he'd hated any kind of conflict, which, if she was totally honest, had made him rather dull company sometimes.

Julien, on the other hand, fired something inside her like no one else she'd ever met.

'Okay, well, I guess this is goodbye then,' she said, standing up on unsteady legs. 'It's been good getting to know you, Julien.' She held out her hand, hoping the tremble in it wasn't too obvious.

He stared down at it for the longest time, before clearing his throat and looking back up, straight into her eyes.

Her stomach swooped at the intensity she saw there.

'Listen, why don't you come out on the boat with me this evening? As—what do you English say?—a last hurrah? We can weigh anchor just off the coast, then you can swim away from the crowds. It would be good to have company for one more evening, to give me a chance to check out the boat before I set off on my lone voyage.'

She froze and stared back at him, excited by the invitation, but trying not to let it get the better of her. It was just a sail and a swim he was offering her, nothing more, she reminded herself sternly.

'That sounds like heaven, but are you sure you don't want some peace after having me chewing your ear off all day?'

He smiled, his lopsided grin shooting a disconcerting dart of desire through her. '*Non*. I enjoyed our discussions today. It was a nice distraction.' He didn't say from what, but then he didn't need to. He'd already made it plain why he was here. As an escape from bad memories. Just like her.

'Anyway, I need more time to convince you to give my favourite thriller author another chance,' he continued when she didn't respond immediately. 'I feel I'd be neglecting my duty to you as a friend if I didn't give it at least one more try.'

The word 'friend' jolted her, reinforcing her resolution not to read anything more into this offer.

Despite her concerns, she couldn't bring herself to say no. Not if saying yes meant being around him for a little while longer. She loved the idea that he'd enjoyed her company today and right now she'd take gratification whichever way it came. After Gavin's accusations, it was nice to feel like she had more to offer than just a shoulder to cry on.

'Well, that would be amazing. I tell you what— since the rest of my money's turned up, I'll buy us dinner,' she suggested, needing to retain a modicum of control in their strange non-relationship relationship.

He smiled again, this time with real warmth, the action of it lighting up his whole face. 'Agreed. Then we're even,' he said.

This time she had to force herself to smile back, because, of course, the sad truth was that they wouldn't be.

Not even close.

A couple of hours later, they were sitting at a table in a beachside restaurant with views across its private golden-sand cove, groaning with pleasure after stuffing themselves full of what they both agreed was the best pasta dish they'd had since arriving in Italy.

'I have to try and persuade them to give me the recipe for this so I can teach my evening class how to make it,' Indigo said, looking round to see whether she could catch the eye of the waiter.

'Give it a go,' Julien said with a smile. 'Just widen those amazingly persuasive eyes at him and I'm sure he'll do anything you ask.'

He wouldn't be at all surprised if she managed to do it either. Indigo had such a lovely way about her it was almost impossible not to give in to her charms—as he himself had discovered time and time again this week.

'Ha! If only it were that easy,' she replied, her cheeks flushing.

Looking at her now, he realised that talking and bantering with her today had been the most fun he'd had in a very long time. She'd ignited something in him with her quick wit and ability to best his arguments, and he'd grown to like her more and more as the day had passed.

She was excellent company.

That was why he'd suggested she join him for a swim from the boat when he'd realised they were about to part ways back at her hotel. It didn't seem like the right way to end things after they'd had such a good day together.

And he hated loose ends.

They were both quiet for a moment as they watched the waiter bustling about between the busy tables.

'So where are we picking up this boat of yours?'

she asked, turning to look towards where a number of them bobbed out on the open sea.

'Just over there.' He nodded over towards the other side of the cove where small rowboats and motorboats were being rented out to eager tourists.

'You know, I feel like this holiday has turned a corner,' she said, sitting back in her chair with a grin. 'Only a few days ago it was looking like I was going to have to sing for my supper and look at me now. I couldn't ask for more than this.'

When she looked round at him his heart nearly leapt out of his chest at the expression in her eyes. She looked happy. And the thought that perhaps he'd had something to do with that shook him to the core.

Get a grip, man.

'Anyway—' she cleared her throat '—I guess I'd better settle up.' She turned to catch the waiter's eye and make the international hand sign for the bill. 'Then we can go and cool off in the sea.'

That sounded like a very good idea to him right about then.

* * *

A short while after that they sat on a white sofa
at back of the yacht that Julien had chartered,
drinking from bottles of ice-cold beer.

Indigo leaned back against the plump cushions
and stared up at the cloudless sky, barely able to
believe where she was right now.

'You know, when you said *boat*, I envisaged
something more like one of those,' she said,
pointing towards a small rowboat being paddled
back to the shore by a hot-and-bothered-looking
young man while his girlfriend lay back, blithely
trailing her fingers through the water.

'This is more like a luxury cruise liner, albeit a miniature one,' she added, flashing him
a teasing grin.

She'd been speechless when they'd zoomed
across the water by motorboat towards this sleek,
handsome yacht, which she'd assumed must be-
long to some millionaire playboy.

It had a kitchen aboard, for goodness' sake,
and a full-sized bathroom.

And a bedroom.

That last discovery had thrown her for a complete loop.

'So are you going to sleep here tonight?' she asked, trying not to sound as covetous as she felt. It had to be wonderful to be lulled to sleep by the gentle rock and bob of a boat on the ocean. Especially if Julien was there in the bed too.

Don't go there...

'That's the plan,' he replied, taking another long pull on his beer. 'Don't worry, I can take you back to shore in the motorboat any time you want.'

'I'm not worried,' she said. And she wasn't. Not about him getting her safely back to shore anyway. She felt totally safe in his company; there was something very solid and steady about him—reassuring. But when it came to the way she felt about him, the way her heart leapt and her stomach plunged every time he looked at her...well, that was another matter.

And there was something disconcertingly intimate about the two of them being here, alone together, in the middle of the sea.

They sat back, admiring the view in silence, watching the seagulls wheel above them as the sun's final rays transformed into the warm glow of dusk.

'I can't believe they wouldn't give me the recipe for that dish,' she said for the umpteenth time since leaving the restaurant, using her annoyance at not being able to charm the waiter as a way to disguise her twanging nerves. 'And I gave him a really big tip,' she added contritely.

'Ah, well, you can't blame them for keeping the secret of their success close to their chests,' Julien said, employing a full-on Gallic shrug, which made her smile.

'Yeah. I guess it's fair enough,' she grumbled. 'I could probably guess most of the ingredients anyway. I'm going to have to experiment when I get home.'

The thought of home made her chest contract. She didn't want to think about leaving here now that she was having such a good time. Or the fact that she'd probably never see Julien again once she left Italy.

'How's your beer?' he asked, breaking into her thoughts.

'Amazing. Best beer I've ever tasted,' she replied truthfully. She didn't often drink beer, usually opting for a glass of crisp, dry white wine when she went out, but it tasted perfect to her right then. In fact, thinking about it, everything tasted or felt or smelled that much more intensely satisfying when Julien was around. It was as if he made all her senses sit up and pay attention. Whenever she was near him she experienced this constant prickling frisson, as if she was plugged into a low-level electric socket, which made her heart race and her limbs twitch. It was as if her body was priming itself for something to happen. Something momentous and life-changing.

But she was a fool if she thought it would. The frustration of this awareness only made the restlessness worse. It made her want to leap around or jump off something, just to relieve the tension of her unsatisfied need.

'I've been meaning to ask—why the red hair?' Julien asked, reaching out and smoothing a piece of it between his fingers.

The tingle of awareness grew more intense. 'It makes me feel powerful,' she replied, desperately trying to latch on to some of that power to give her the strength to keep her wits about her.

'That figures. It suits you.' He smiled right into her eyes, making her breath hitch in her throat.

She gave a little cough to clear the tension. 'Thanks. I've wanted to do it for a while, but Gavin, my ex, wasn't keen, so I didn't until just before I came here.'

His eyebrows nearly hit his hairline. 'Really? I was under the impression you don't like to take orders from anyone.'

Huffing out a laugh, she pulled her feet up on to the sofa and hugged her knees to her. 'I don't normally. But whenever I brought it up as an idea he accused me of not taking his feelings into consideration and I felt bad about that.'

She looked away, remembering the frustration she used to feel when Gavin laid on the guilt to get his own way. It nearly always ended up with her giving in to what he wanted when he did that.

That was something she didn't miss.

Come to think of it, the hurt she'd been carrying around at the beginning of the week seemed to be greatly reduced now. Perhaps it had something to do with having something new and exciting to concentrate on.

Or someone.

Stop!

'Okay, I'm going for a swim before it gets too dark,' she said, springing up, unable to sit still next to Julien any longer, making him jerk in surprise.

Before he could say a word, she dashed down the steps to the diving platform, pulled off the towel she'd wrapped around her to cover her bikini and dived into the water.

The shock of the cold water was a delicious relief against her heated skin, and her heartbeat begin to calm as she swam steadily away from the boat, riding the gentle dip and swell of the waves, feeling a corresponding lift in her tummy.

In the distance, the cliffs rose majestically before her, the foliage vividly green against the soft grey of the rock.

It was so peaceful here, on her own in the middle of the sea with the vast sky above her and the undulating water disappearing into the horizon. This withdrawal was exactly what she needed right now to soothe the raging noise in her head.

It had been fine being alone with Julien when they were walking. The constant forward motion and changing scenery had kept her mind distracted from the intensity of his nearness, but now they were stuck in one place together she was afraid she wouldn't be able to hide how he made her feel when she was around him.

Deep inside her head she knew—she *knew*—that Julien wasn't emotionally available right now and that she should accept that as fact. He'd certainly warned her about it enough times, but it didn't stop her from wondering—hoping—*what if?*

When she finally forced herself to look back towards the boat, she saw that Julien was standing on the diving platform, his face turned towards her, shielding his eyes against the last low rays of the sun.

'Are you coming in? It feels wonderful!' she shouted, aware that her pulse had picked up again at the discovery that he'd been watching her all this time.

He paused for a moment and she got the distinct impression he was searching for an excuse not to join her, but apparently he thought better of it, pulling his T-shirt over his head in one deft move and stepping up on to the edge of the boat.

Indigo trod water, feeling her body being lifted and dropped by the gentle waves as she stared in rapt delight at his muscular physique, immensely glad of the cooling effect of the water as her body surged with nervous heat.

He dived in with the same grace he applied to every physical action and swam towards her, powering through the water. When he reached her, he stopped, barely touching distance away and gave her a wide grin.

'You're right; it does feel wonderful.'

She smiled back, wishing with all her heart that it was okay for her to reach out to him, to slide into his arms and wrap her legs around his waist, to ride the waves with him and laugh and play, then kiss him hard, so he'd know how much she was enjoying being here with him. How he'd opened up this whole new sense of excitement for life in her that she so desperately wanted to cling on to.

For this to be *their* holiday.

She longed to ask him how he'd feel about

spending the rest of his week with her, but she knew she'd be on dangerous ground. This link between them was so tenuous it would snap as soon as she put any kind of pressure on it.

So instead, in an attempt to relieve her frustration and wipe that easy smile off his face, she drew back her hand and swished a sheet of water at him.

He didn't see it coming and got a face full.

'Right!' he said with an ominous growl after he'd recovered from the surprise of it, wiping the water off his face with an expression that promised retaliation.

She shrieked and swam away from him, turning back to find him in hot pursuit.

They laughed and played like a couple of kids, chasing each other through the water and sending great sprays of water back and forth until Indigo held up her hand in defeat, her eyes now stinging from the make-up she'd forgotten to take off before jumping into the water.

'Ow, ow, ow! My eyes! Wait, Julien, wait, I

can't see.' Distracted by the smarting pain, she forgot to kick and dipped down into the water, sucking in a mouthful of it.

Kicking back up in alarm, she spluttered, coughing the water out and wincing at the revolting taste.

'Are you okay?' she heard Julien say, somewhere close by.

She nodded, but proved herself wrong by accidentally taking in another gulp of briny water when she drew in a breath to try and cough the sharpness out of her throat, starting to panic as she felt herself sinking back down beneath the waves again.

'It's okay, I've got you,' he said right next to her now.

She felt his arm slide around her waist and he pulled her securely against his chest, lifting her further out of the water. She clung to him, wrapping her legs around his hips to make it easier for him to swim, and he kicked hard, quickly taking them the few metres back to the boat.

Reaching to grab hold of the rail at the stern, he hauled them both on to the diving platform and they toppled backwards with the momentum, Indigo landing on her back beneath him.

He looked down at her, his face only inches from hers, his eyes dark with alarm.

'Are you okay?' he asked, the concern in his voice making her shiver.

She was suddenly acutely aware of how little clothing she was wearing and how solid and warm the boat's deck was under her back and how good the hard press of his body felt between her legs.

All she could do was nod in response.

'You look like a bedraggled panda,' he murmured, his voice sounding rough and deep as he ran his thumbs gently under her eyes, wiping the make-up away.

The simple tenderness of this action undid her and, from out of nowhere, an overwhelming urge to cry hit her, forcing the air from her lungs and tightening her throat. But she didn't want to let the tears come. Not like this, not with him looking at her like he was. He'd see it—her vulnerability and need. So, in the absence of a better idea, she raised her head those few precious inches and kissed him.

In her head, she'd meant it to be a kiss of gratitude, an apology to smooth away his worry, an acknowledgement of his act of kindness, but as soon as her lips touched his, she was lost.

She let out a small moan as she registered the firmness of his mouth, then a gasp as his lips parted so she could sweep the tip of her tongue against his.

He tasted so good: musky and seductive and sweet all wrapped up into one delicious essence. Pressing her lips harder against his, she tightened her grip and pulled his body closer to her, so she was hard up against his solid chest, revelling in the strength of him as she wrapped her limbs around him.

She was drowning again, only this time in his scent, turning into a bundle of nerve endings under his touch. Her whole body sang with joy as she felt the power of him surround her, drawing her down deep into the oblivion of the kiss.

Until something changed.

Her heart started to hammer as she realised he was withdrawing from her.

'Wait, Indigo, stop,' he muttered against her mouth, lifting himself away so she had to loosen her grip on him.

Misery sank through her in a heavy wave as she realised what she'd done.

Exactly what she'd been warning herself against for the entire day.

She'd given herself away again.

When she dared to open her eyes, he was shaking his head, his eyes squeezed tightly closed as if he was trying to will away what had just happened.

And then, like before, when laughter had overtaken her, something seemed to snap inside, only this time it was the tears that came, racking her body with brutal sobs.

'I'm sorry, I'm so sorry,' she managed to struggle out between gasps, wishing she was anywhere but there with Julien right then. She hated him seeing her break down like this.

'I guess I'm still feeling a bit raw and lonely after Gavin dumped me like he did. Not that that's much of an excuse.'

His dismayed expression told her everything she needed to know. She'd totally blown it with him now.

'Stay here. I'll go and get us some towels,' he said, getting up awkwardly.

She felt the cool movement of air on her skin as he left her, which was immediately replaced by the hot sting of humiliation.

Sitting up, she rolled on to her knees then carefully got to her feet, not entirely sure her legs were going to hold her up.

No way was she going to cower here like an idiot until he returned.

By the time she walked on to the main deck, he was coming back with two large, fluffy white towels. He handed one to her and used the other to wipe the remaining water from his face.

'Thank you,' she said, wrapping it tightly around her, unable to make eye contact with him.

'Indigo? Are you okay?' he asked quietly.

When she finally plucked up the courage to look at him his expression was dark with frustration.

'I'm just going to go and wash my face,' she said, tearing her gaze away and turning to make her way shakily down to the belly of the boat.

In the bathroom she sat down on the closed toilet seat and dropped her head into her hands.

What a fool she was. And she only had herself to blame. She'd thought she could handle being here with him—that it wouldn't mean anything to her, but it did. It did.

It meant the world to her.

After washing away the remainder of the make-up, she took a deep bolstering breath and left the bathroom, deciding to ask Julien to take her back to shore right now, before things got any more awkward between them—if that was even possible.

She found him sitting on the sofa when she shuffled back on to the deck, his elbows on his knees and his hands clasped in front of him. He hadn't bothered putting his T-shirt back on and his bare chest glinted with water droplets in the final dying rays of the sun.

Another tormenting rush of awareness made her skin tingle from head to toe.

She perched on the edge of the sofa next to him, readying herself to make some excuse about being tired or needing to get up early the next morning so he wouldn't have to feel guilty about getting her off his boat as soon as possible.

Acutely aware that this would be the last time she'd ever see him, she took a breath and turned to face him, her throat tight with sorrow.

'Tell me what happened with your ex,' he said before she had chance to speak, regarding her with a furrowed brow.

She stared at him, wondering whether she'd misheard.

He just looked back at her with an expectant expression on his face.

'Are—are you sure you want to hear it?' she stuttered.

'*Oui.*'

His genuine concern lit a fire within her, warming her both inside and out, but still she hesitated, not sure she wanted him to know the full humiliating story.

He held up a finger. 'Wait. I'll get us more beer.'

Returning a moment later with two more bottles of ice-cold beer, he handed one to her and sat back down, clinking the neck of his against hers before taking a long swallow and raising his eyebrows at her expectantly, waiting for her to begin.

She could *not* tell him, of course—could make up some general non-specific story about things not working out between her and Gavin—but she respected Julien too much to fob him off like that.

She took a long drink from her own bottle, then sat back and took a steadying breath, fighting back the nerves in her tummy before she spoke.

'Apparently my ex, Gavin, needed to be with someone who was more grateful to have him as a boyfriend.'

'More grateful?' Julien repeated slowly, looking thunderstruck.

She sighed and spread out her hands on her lap, staring down at them for courage.

'Yes, well, our relationship was a bit strange. We met when he needed somewhere to stay after his wife told him she wanted a divorce, and I had a spare room available, so I offered it to him as a stopgap—as a favour to a friend of a friend. He was an emotional wreck when he moved in and I made a huge effort to make him feel as welcome as possible.' She took a breath. 'We ended up getting really close and things sort of developed between us…romantically.'

She glanced at Julien but he just nodded.

'I really liked being the one he leaned on for support. I guess it fed into my need to try and fix people, or at least make their lives easier. I'd lost my dad six months before, after years of looking after him, and I felt a bit adrift. Gavin was the first serious boyfriend I'd ever had and I really threw myself into being with him.' She looked away, across towards the darkening horizon.

'I guess I feel drawn to looking after people. It's what I do. It makes me feel happy. Useful. In control—or something.' She knew she sounded defensive, but Julien didn't react so she kept talking.

'Everything was okay between Gavin and me until I started the Welcome Café,' she continued, wanting Julien to have the whole story before he judged her.

'He wanted to give me advice about how to run it—he has his own catering business—and he used to get really offended if I didn't do what he suggested.'

Julien went to speak but she held up a hand, asking him to wait.

'To be fair to him, I'd started spending a lot of evenings working late and at the weekends, so I guess he must have felt neglected as well as ignored.' She sighed and rubbed a hand over her face, vaguely aware of how tight her skin felt after her dip in the sea.

'Thinking about it now, I can see the signs I missed. He'd been frustrated with me at the end of last year because he'd wanted me to go to parties and networking events with him, but I'd made commitments at work that I couldn't get out of so I hadn't been able to go to them.'

Balancing the bottle on her knee, she twisted the neck in her fingers. 'Then, three months ago, I found an engagement ring in the pocket of his coat and got all excited about it being for me.' The familiar tension began to build at the base of her spine.

'He walked into the hall while I was standing there with a goofy smile on my face, staring at it. He went totally white. Like all the blood had drained from his face. At first I thought it was because I'd ruined the surprise by finding the ring before he'd had chance to set up the proposal, but the look in his eyes told me otherwise.'

She realigned the bottle so that the label faced her square-on, unable to look at Julien now, humiliation burning her cheeks.

'He'd bought it to propose to the woman he'd been cheating on me with.' She stared harder at the beer bottle, catching a drip of condensation on her fingertip as it made its way down the neck. 'He said he was going to tell me when he'd figured out the kindest way to break it to me, but I guess fate stepped in and forced his hand.'

She made an exploding motion with her hands. 'And that was the end of our relationship. They're getting married on Christmas Day, apparently. A winter wedding. Very romantic.'

Looking away, she tested the cool base of the empty bottle against the prickling palm of her hand to distract herself from how hot with mortification she suddenly felt.

'He didn't even give me a chance to fix what I was doing wrong—just found someone else and moved on.'

'It sounds like there wasn't anything for you to fix. He was a coward who used you to get back on his feet—taking advantage of your keen sense of compassion—then cheated on you because he's weak and selfish,' Julien said. There was a rough edge to his voice that she hadn't heard before.

Determined not to give in to the humiliation pressing at the edges of her mind, she sat up on the sofa and gave him a smile, which she hoped came across with sufficient sangfroid. 'Yeah, maybe that's how I should look at it.'

He was looking at her now with a strange expression on his face. Something like solidarity. Or affection.

Or perhaps that was just what she wanted it to be.

Oh, how she ached for it to be that. And more, so much more.

'According to him, it was my fault because I'd started to treat him like a project I'd grown bored with.'

'Had you? Grown bored with him?'

'No.' She shrugged, then sighed in exasperation. 'I don't know. Maybe. I never meant him to feel like that. But I guess once he didn't need me as much any more I took a step back. Perhaps he didn't like the fact I stopped doting on him like I had previously.'

'You mean you started concentrating on yourself and the café and he was annoyed that he'd lost your undivided attention.'

'I guess.' The mention of the café reminded her what was waiting for her to deal with when she got back home, making her stomach roll with unease. 'Ironically, I might lose the café soon anyway if we don't get the funding we need. It can't afford to pay me a living wage for much longer if we don't get the grant I've applied for, and there's no way I'm going to fire any of my staff when they've worked so hard to make it a success.'

Putting the bottle back to her lips, she was surprised to find she'd almost finished. Shrugging, she knocked back the last bit, then stared out towards the twinkling lights that had begun to appear through the velvety dusk in nearby Nerano, desperately trying to pull herself together and regain some modicum of pride.

Julien stared at Indigo's profile, transfixed, as she gazed off into the distance, the pain of her admission clear on her face. She looked younger and more vulnerable without the benefit of her make-up, and the sight of it touched something in his heart.

There was a tight pressure in his chest as he reflected on all that she'd told him. She blamed herself for the breakup of her relationship, which was patently ridiculous. It sounded like the guy hadn't been man enough to handle someone as headstrong as Indigo and, instead of having an honest conversation with her, he'd lied and cheated as a way to escape from a situation he couldn't control.

A raging sense of injustice made him move closer to her on the sofa and slide his hand under her jaw, gently urging her to turn back and face him. He wanted to say something, do something to take that look from her face.

'It never would have worked with Gavin, you know,' he said, shocked by the force of his words as they left his lips.

She blanched, her eyes widening, clearly surprised by the vehemence of his statement. 'You don't think so?'

'*Non.*'

'Why not?'

'Because you emasculated him.'

'What? What do you mean?' Pulling away

from his touch, she stood up and took a step away from him.

He stood up too and held out a placating hand. 'I mean he sounds like the type of guy that needs his partner to dote on him to make him feel powerful.' He hadn't meant to alarm her, but he could tell from her body language that he had.

She blinked at him, hurt flashing in her eyes. 'You think I took his power away?'

'Not intentionally, I'm sure. Lots of men can't handle being with smart, assertive women.'

'Great. So what you're telling me is that, basically, if I want to run my own business I'm destined to be single forever.'

He made a move towards her, then stopped himself. 'I didn't say that.'

Her foot slid a little on the deck as she took another step backwards. 'I can't change the way I am, Julien.'

'You don't have to.'

He moved so he was standing right in front of her, barely inches away, and waited until she looked him in the eye again before he spoke. He felt a fierce, instinctive desire to let her know what an incredible person she was.

'Indigo, you're a very attractive woman. Clever, courageous, generous. You'll have no problem finding the right person to love you. Your ex was a fool not to appreciate you.'

She swallowed hard. 'You think? None of those things seem to impress you enough either. You can't even bring yourself to kiss me.' Folding her arms across her chest, she stared down at the floor.

He sighed and rubbed a hand over his face. 'That's because things are complicated for me at the moment.'

She raised a hand. 'It's okay, you don't have to make an excuse. I get it.'

'No, you *don't*, Indigo. You don't get it at all. You're the sexiest, most alluring woman I've ever met, but—'

Unfolding her arms, she flung her hands in the air. 'There's always a "but"!'

'Oui.' He lifted a hand to cup her chin again and force her to look at him so she could see the regret on his face. 'There is.'

His heart thumped heavily against his ribs as he stared into her striking eyes, her pupils so blown he could barely make out the dark ring of her irises in the sinking gloom.

It would feel so good to kiss her right now, to take away her pain. But he knew there would be no going back from it, but also no going forward. He shouldn't put her through that, not when she'd been hurt like she had.

So he just stood there like a fool, inhibited by a powerful sense of walking to the edge of a cliff and looking down into the depths, feeling an innate urge to jump.

'Take me back to shore, Julien. It's time we said goodbye,' she murmured, her eyes welling with fresh tears.

Taking a shuddering breath, she plucked at the end of the towel, which was still wrapped tightly around her, lifting up the edge and using it to dry her eyes before looking up at him again.

His heart gave a hard pulse in his chest at the sight of the pain and humiliation he saw in them.

Because of him.

Seeming to read his concern, she dropped her chin and stared at the floor. 'I'm sorry. I think I drank too much after being teetotal all week. And I'm tired. So tired.' She seemed to sag, as if all the fight had left her, and on instinct he pulled her into a tight hug against him, finding comfort in the scent of her that had become so familiar to him over the last few days. Strangely, he felt as if he'd known it forever.

And they fitted so well together. Like two pieces of a puzzle.

Relaxing his hold on her, he moved back a little so he could look into her face.

'Stay here on the boat tonight,' he heard himself saying.

'What?' Her expression was so full of wounded confusion he knew there was no way he could let her leave now. He had this fierce urge to protect and comfort her, even if it was only for one night.

'I want you to stay with me tonight. Let me prove to you exactly how attractive I find you.'

Without letting her utter another word, he bent to claim her mouth with his own, his body shivering with desire as he experienced the incredible soft sweetness of her again.

Now he'd made the decision he wanted her so much it hurt.

Before she could protest, he scooped her up into his arms, making for the steps to below deck where the bedroom was housed.

The sound of her giggle was music to his ears. 'Julien, you don't need to carry me. I can walk!'

He ignored her, striding down to the forepeak of the boat and into the bedroom, where he lay her gently on the bed.

'Let me look after you tonight, Indigo,' he said, brushing the hair away from her face and settling in next to her, dipping his head to claim her mouth once again.

She gave a small groan of need in the back of her throat. 'Yes,' she whispered against his lips, wrapping her arms around him.

And that was all he needed to hear to finally let himself go.

CHAPTER EIGHT

Nerano to Sorrento. Walking away from Nerano will be hard, but the cheering lure of Sorrento calls...

WHEN INDIGO WOKE up she couldn't quite place where she was. Opening her eyes a crack, all she saw was a plain white wall, which swooped up towards the ceiling like a roof in an attic room. Strange. She didn't remember going to bed in an attic.

Coming round a little more, she became aware of an unfamiliar rocking motion beneath her and a heavy weight around her waist that pressed gently into her tummy. Despite her disorientation, she felt curiously safe and protected.

Even so, something in the back of her brain told her that this wasn't where she was supposed to be, and as she shifted a little she felt a warm pressure behind her sink a little harder into her back.

Okay, that definitely wasn't right.

Holding her breath, she turned over carefully so as not to disturb whatever was behind her, only to find herself face to face with Julien. His eyes were still firmly shut and flickering slightly in REM sleep, his chest bare above the covers.

It all came flooding back to her in one long agonising rush.

She'd totally lost it last night after telling Julien all her sorry woes and he'd felt forced into taking her to bed to comfort her.

Ugh! What a fool she'd made of herself.

Poor Julien. He'd invited her for a sail and swim from his boat and she'd gone all melodramatic talk show on him.

Trouble was, she'd been holding in this guilt—this fear that the failure of the relationship with Gavin had all been her fault—for so long she'd not realised how close to the surface her pain and sadness really was. She'd just kept pushing it down in order to survive, and as soon as anyone had shown the slightest bit of interest in her she'd blurted the whole thing out in one long rambling splurge.

And he'd been so kind about it. In fact, he'd been more than kind, he'd been downright generous in his praise of her. Which had only served to heighten the emotion of it all.

It had been like catharsis, hearing Julien—someone she respected, revered and whose opinion she cared about—tell her it wasn't her fault. It had released something inside her. She'd finally been able to let the shame go and see the bigger picture.

It had brought it home to her what a fool she'd been thinking that Gavin could be someone she could spend the rest of her life with. She'd had a lucky escape when he left her.

Winter Wedding Woman was welcome to him and his inferiority complex.

But watching Julien now as he slept so peacefully, she felt like a fraud. She'd let him think she was distraught about Gavin leaving her, but that hadn't really been it at all. It was Julien she was most upset about. As she'd told him her miserable tale and seen the understanding and support in his eyes she'd known without a doubt that she'd lied to herself about their connection meaning nothing important to her.

She was in love with him.

Truly and desperately.

But of course she knew it was pointless to hope he felt the same way. He'd already backed away from her more than once, citing his need for freedom after his messy divorce, and one night with her wasn't going to change that.

After the pain of Gavin's cruel dismissal she couldn't put herself in a position where she'd be rejected like that again. Not unless Julien gave her a sign that he'd changed his mind about not looking for another relationship, which she was pretty sure he wasn't going to do.

He'd probably only slept with her last night

because he'd felt sorry for her and didn't know what else to do when she'd blubbed all over him.

Her whole body flooded with prickly heat at the thought.

Was that all it had been? A kindness to her? Because he *was* kind—she knew that now she'd finally broken through his gruff exterior. But he'd probably regret what they'd done this morning.

She stared into his handsome face, wondering what it would be like to wake up every day and find him lying next to her. To be allowed to reach over and cup his face in her hands and plant a tender loving kiss on his lips. To be grateful every day for his presence beside her.

There was an ache deep inside her ribs that was making it hard to breathe. The hopelessness of the situation made her want to scream with frustration. Why did she have to meet him now? At the worst possible time in his life.

Perhaps because it wasn't meant to be, a small voice in her head warned.

If only he'd lower his defences enough for her to get through to him. But she understood why he was afraid to let her in; divorce could be a soul-destroying experience that could take months or even years to recover from. And with him living so far away from her there would be no opportunity to take things slowly, to try each other out for size, without making a major commitment.

It would be asking way too much of him.

And she wasn't prepared to be just some woman he'd had a fling with on the rebound.

She knew how these things went. He'd forget all about her once he returned to his real life, once the enchantment of the holiday had worn off. She'd just be some girl he once knew for a few days. An interlude. Barely even an anecdote.

Whereas for her, meeting Julien had been the best thing that had ever happened to her.

As if her last piercing thought had penetrated his dreams, Julien's eyes began to flicker open and he blinked hard, his pupils dilating as he stared into her face in confusion.

For just one heart-stopping second she thought he might lean forwards and kiss her, but he seemed to pull himself together and come fully awake, his brow creasing into a frown.

'Good morning, Indigo, how are you feeling today?'

God, she loved how he said her name, as if he was stroking every syllable with his tongue.

A telltale warmth crept up her neck at the rogue thought, continuing upwards to flush her face with heat.

'A little embarrassed if I'm honest,' she said, averting her eyes from his searching gaze.

He shifted back away from her and sat up, swinging his legs over the edge of the bed.

Realising how disrespectful that sounded, she put out a hand to touch the smooth skin of his back, but withdrew it quickly before she made contact. It felt like too intimate a gesture. 'I mean, I'm sorry for crying on you last night.'

Half turning back to face her, he exhaled in a rush of breath and shook his head.

'No apology necessary. I had fun.'

A bit of fun. That was all it had been.

A feeling of cold acceptance flooded through her, as if the remains of her hope was being washed away, leaving her thoughts clean and jagged.

Hardening the last piece of her heart, she leant down and plucked the towel that she'd been wearing last night from the floor and sat up to wrap it tightly around her.

'Well, I suppose I really ought to get back to shore. I want to get to Sorrento before the end of the day so I can have a good look around before setting off for Capri the day after. Could you take me back in the motorboat, please?'

Her words sounded so perfunctory she cringed with unease.

When she turned to look at him he was staring at her in confused surprise, then blinked and nodded as if coming out of a trance when he saw she was looking at him. '*Oui*. Okay.'

'Thank you.'

Not daring to look at him again, she strode quickly out of the room and into the bathroom, where she'd left her clothes the previous evening after getting changed into her bikini, trying to ignore the voices in her head that were urging her to turn around and tell him that she'd changed her mind and that she could stay for a little longer. Just till they'd eaten breakfast together.

Pull yourself together, Indigo, you fool! You're not a couple and you never will be.

Pulling on the dress she'd chosen with such care for their dinner together last night, she turned to the mirror to try and do something with her hair. It was sticking up in all directions after she'd slept on it wet and refused to play ball, so after a minute of fruitless fussing she gave up on it. She was desperate for a shower, but now that she'd made her mind up to go she didn't want to linger. It would only prolong the pain of leaving.

Giving her puffy face one last dismayed look in the mirror, she left the bathroom and made her way to the living area, where she found Julien sitting on the sofa waiting for her.

He stood up quickly when he saw her and walked with her towards the door to the upper deck, neither of them saying a word.

'Wait.' He put an arm across the doorway before she could walk through it, blocking her way out.

Her heart hammered hard in her chest as she looked up into his mesmerising eyes.

'You know, Indigo, if you don't mind missing that part of the walk I can sail you to Sorrento, then pick you up again the next day and drop you in Capri. I'm going that way anyway. You may as well come along for the ride.'

It was so tempting. But what a ride it would be. Just the thought of having to put a brave face on for him, pretending she was fine with them just being casual lovers for the next couple of days, made her shudder with horror.

No, she'd be better to cut her losses now and walk away while she still had some of her wits about her.

'No. Thanks. To be honest, I don't want to miss walking that bit of the track.' She couldn't meet his eyes. 'I only have a couple of days left here before it's time to get back to reality and I'm sure you don't really want me tagging along for the rest of your holiday.'

He was frowning at her now, which wasn't surprising as her voice seemed to have morphed into that of an ailing crow again.

'Are you sure you're okay?' he asked with real concern in his voice.

'Yes. I was just thinking about what you said about Gavin.'

'*Oui?*' He looked uncomfortable at the mention of her ex.

'I think you're right; it would never have worked out with him long term. I've been so distracted by the pain and humiliation of the way he dumped me I got the feeling muddled with missing him. I need to be with someone who's proud of me for what I've achieved, not jealous of my success. I've been beating myself up about the wrong things. It's time I stopped.'

'*Oui.*'

'Thank you, for making me realise that.'

'You're welcome. You deserve to be happy, Indigo.'

'As do you, Julien.'

They stared at each other, with the crackle of unsaid words in the air around them.

Say something more, Julien. Please.

But he didn't; he just nodded in a sage kind of way, as if he hadn't heard the underlying pleading in her voice.

So that was it; she had to leave right now, on her terms. It was important for her peace of mind that she kept her control, after having it so savagely ripped away from her in her last relationship.

For her own sense of self-confidence, she couldn't allow Julien to dismiss her too.

'Okay, well, I'm ready to go when you are,' she said overly brightly.

He didn't say another word as they walked up to the deck together. When they reached where the small onboard motorboat was housed, she hung back until he'd released it from its mooring and manoeuvred it down the small slope and into the water.

After climbing in he held out his hand to help her climb in too and she hoped to goodness he wouldn't notice how much she was shaking.

Neither of them said a word as Julien piloted the small craft back to the shore, sending waves of froth into the choppy water behind them.

At any other time she would have loved the feeling of powering through the waves at high speed, revelling in the adrenaline rush of something so alien and exciting, but the heavy tug of gloom in her belly cancelled out any enjoyment she might have felt.

Julien drove the boat straight on to the deserted beach and jumped out, pulling it further ashore so she could step out without getting her feet wet.

Hopping out, she turned to face him.

'So, I guess this is it then,' she said, turning to give him a smile that she knew must look incredibly fake.

'Probably not,' he said, dipping his chin and raising his eyebrow, his eyes holding a look she couldn't decipher.

Was he making a joke about their strangely magnetic connection, or was he about to ask to see her again after he'd concluded his holiday?

She drew in a shaky breath, anticipation making a pulse beat hard in her throat.

'Based on our luck so far, we're bound to run into each other on Capri,' he said with a playful lilt to his voice.

She nodded and waited—heart racing, breath stuck in her throat—for him to suggest they made a plan to meet up there.

But he didn't. Instead, he gave her a tight smile, then turned to look back towards where his yacht was anchored a mile or so off the coast. 'Well, I'd better get back and chart my course,' he said, his voice giving no suggestion at all that he was sorry to see her go. 'I only have the boat for three more days then it's back to real life.'

Real life.

Her stomach dipped and her eyes grew hot, but she refused to show him how much it was going to hurt her to leave him like this.

'Okay, well, enjoy the rest of your holiday,' she said, steeling herself as he moved towards her and placed a gentle kiss on each cheek, French-style.

'It was good knowing you, Indigo,' he murmured into her ear, before pulling back and giving her a firm nod.

'You too, Julien.' She was amazed she'd been able to get the words past her throat.

He nodded once more before turning abruptly on the spot and striding away from her.

* * *

It felt empty on the boat after Indigo had gone.

Julien paced up and down the deck feeling unsettled about the way she'd left so suddenly.

When he'd woken up to find her watching him with that perplexed expression in her eyes, he'd been worried that he'd made a huge mistake asking her to stay the night, that he'd hurt her more than helped her—and set himself up for more heartache too—and his first instinct had been to gently let her know that it had been a one-time-only thing for him.

He'd been relieved when she'd made the decision to go without him having to say anything, but he'd also been taken aback and a little perturbed by how vehement she'd been about it.

Something about the way she'd sprung out of bed didn't sit well with him.

After that he'd felt compelled to offer her a lift to Sorrento and had experienced a strange sting of hurt when she'd been almost cold in her refusal.

The memory of it disturbed him.

Perhaps she'd been embarrassed about what had happened between them after she'd fallen apart last night.

He wasn't, though. He'd loved the feel of her in his arms and the softness of her pressed beneath him. She'd been so responsive to him, making it clear she'd enjoyed his touch as much as he'd enjoyed hers.

Maybe she was just distracted by the thought of what awaited her when she got home after talking to him about it last night.

It made him so angry to think about how badly her ex had treated her because her strength and tenacity had intimidated him. And he hated the idea that she had to deal with the threat of the business she'd worked so hard to build from nothing being taken away from her all by herself.

She deserved better.

Needing a distraction from his thoughts, he went down into the galley kitchen and fixed himself some breakfast, raiding the ready-stocked cupboards and fridge, choosing sugar-free muesli and strong black coffee to satisfy his appetite. Not that he felt particularly hungry this morning.

After clearing away his crockery, he tried reading one of the books from a shelf in the living area, but he couldn't seem to concentrate on it. He was restless and twitchy. Perhaps Indigo had had a point about not missing today's walk. His body seemed attuned to doing that much exercise now and the lack of it today had left him with an abundance of energy.

Getting up, he went down to the bedroom and made the bed, pausing to skim his fingers over a small black smudge that the last of her eye make-up had left on one of the pillows.

It made him think of the way she'd looked at him through her thick black lashes when she wanted him to agree to something and a sudden, disorientating feeling of loss hit him straight in the solar plexus, taking his breath away.

Like the walking, he'd become so attuned to her presence he appeared to be missing her company.

Which finally brought him round to the real reason he'd felt troubled about her leaving so suddenly.

Waking up in the early hours of the morning to find her warm body snuggled up against his had shaken him. Lying there under the heavy blanket of night he'd felt such a sense of calm—for the first time in as long as he could remember. He'd rested there, with Indigo in his arms, exulting in the rush and pull of the ocean beneath them, enjoying the gentle melody of the waves against the hull of the boat as he drifted in and out of sleep.

In his half wakeful state, he'd relived the feel of her long, long limbs wrapped around him, and the intoxicating scent of her as he dragged it deep into his lungs and the sweet taste of her in his mouth. He'd wanted her so badly he ached with it, and he'd just taken what he wanted even though he'd known it was a bad idea. An insight that had been reinforced when he'd seen the regret in her eyes the next morning.

It reminded him a little too keenly of all those gut-wrenching mornings, waking up next to Celine and seeing the shuttered look on her face. The cold, blank expression of a woman who despised him.

His failure to make things right between him and Celine still haunted him, even though they were divorced now and she was no longer his responsibility. He'd always been able to fix things before he met her—by finally earning enough money to buy his mother the kind of house she deserved and provide her with a lifestyle that made her happy, by finding jobs for friends who found themselves adrift and in money trouble—but with Celine he'd not been able to find a way to satisfy her. He'd given her everything he could think of and it still hadn't been enough.

It had eaten away at him.

And now he had a new regret.

He'd known, in his heart, that Indigo wasn't the sort of person who would be satisfied with a one-night stand, but he'd gone ahead and let it happen anyway. To satisfy his greedy need.

Slumping down on to the bed, he rolled on to his back and stared up at the ceiling, imagining the vast blue sky stretching out above him, feeling smaller and more helpless than he was comfortable with.

He really didn't want to have Indigo's suffering gnawing away at him too. He could have done so much more to make her happy, but he'd let her go, telling himself it was what she wanted.

She'd needed more from him than a kiss on the cheek and a metaphorical pat on the head.

His hands twitched at his sides as blood rushed through his veins.

There was no way he could leave things with her like this; it would plague him for the rest of his life.

Especially when he knew he could do something to really help and support her.

Sitting up, he took a deep fortifying breath, feeling his energy returning as purpose and resolve flooded his body with adrenaline.

He was going to find her and make things right.

CHAPTER NINE

Sorrento to Capri. It could be a rough ride between the mainland and the island, so be prepared for turbulence on your journey. Don't worry—once you're there it'll all be worth it...

HE'D NOT BEEN able to find Indigo in Sorrento.

It was ridiculous for him to feel miffed about the fact because the town had a population of over fifteen thousand, which no doubt doubled in high season. But after not being able to avoid her at the beginning of the week he'd fully expected to bump into her as soon as he set foot on dry land.

But after a fruitless search through the town, where he felt as if he'd visited every eatery and hotel that Sorrento had to offer, his heart lurching every time he caught so much as a flash of the colour red, he'd finally given up, deciding the best place to catch her would be the small port in Capri where the ferries sailed in from Sorrento on a regular basis.

Mooring the yacht in the marina just to the west of the main ferry port, he holed up early for the evening, determined to get up at the crack of dawn in order to meet the first ferry of the day in case Indigo was on it.

It felt good to have a purpose after spending the rest of the week in a state of disconnected limbo, occasionally checking his work email for news, only to find that everything was running smoothly without him. This had both heartened and distressed him.

He didn't like the idea of not being needed.

The early morning air felt fresh and cool on his skin as he made his way over to where the passenger ferries docked in the marina, armed with a bag full of food and beverages so he wouldn't

have to run the risk of missing Indigo in between landings.

When he arrived, the place was only just waking up for business, catering for a few early ris-
ers who paced about waiting for the first ferry
to arrive and take them back to the mainland.

He could tell from the intensity of the first
rays of the sun burning through the low hanging
clouds that it was going to be another hot day.

Settling down on to one of the long stone
benches that faced out across the water, he took
out a book he'd borrowed from his yacht's small
library, made himself as comfortable as possible
on a seat that wasn't really designed for people
to sit on for more than a few minutes and prepared himself to wait until Indigo made an appearance.

Since leaving Julien on the beach in Nerano,
Indigo had spent her time making good on her
decision to continue the walk to Sorrento. In a
stroke of pure luck, she'd bumped into Ruth and

her group heading that way too, and was somewhat relieved to find herself warmly integrated back into the group.

She'd needed the distraction after spending the morning in a state of torment after saying goodbye to Julien.

It had taken Ruth a couple of miles' worth of small talk before she finally got round to asking about him, clearly sensing that there was something wrong in Indigo's world but that she wasn't going to bring it up herself.

Indigo had been preparing herself to talk about Julien, but even so, it was still hard to make her story of their walk to Nerano and subsequent night on the yacht sound as inconsequential as she'd wanted it to.

Ruth had not been fooled by her bluster though and had pressed her about their relationship until Indigo had given up on the pretence that he meant nothing important to her and blurted out the whole sorry tale.

'He sounds like he needs more time, love,'

Ruth told her as they walked the last leg towards Sorrento.

'Yeah, I know,' she said with a sigh. 'It was just really bad timing.' They walked for another mile or so in companionable silence, with Indigo's thoughts spinning through her head until she couldn't keep it in any longer.

'I just felt like we were meant to meet,' she blurted. 'It was like some force kept dragging us back together. It felt right to be with him, you know?'

'I do,' Ruth agreed. 'My husband and I met in Western Samoa, of all places, after living only five miles apart for twelve years, never having crossed paths before. We kept missing each other, even though we now realise we'd attended quite a few of the same events. He was married to someone else at the time, though, who sadly died after a long illness a year before he and I met each other in Samoa, so it wouldn't have worked out if we'd bumped into each other earlier. It's funny how these things happen. You can't help but suspect there's some kind of benevolent force pushing you together at the right time.'

'Yeah, but if the other person isn't ready, there's only so much magic fate can weave.'

They'd come to a halt on the outskirts of the town at that point and Ruth put a comforting arm around her. 'If it's meant to be, you'll see him again, honey,' she said with a warmth in her voice that made Indigo think of the cuddles her mum used to give her when she was upset about something. From out of nowhere, she experienced a sudden and intense pang of loss. The grief of losing her mother never seemed to lessen, though it hit her less often these days, usually when she was feeling particularly low. This time it had the disconcerting effect of reminding her just how alone in the world she was right then.

Forcing back the tears that threatened to spill over, she hugged Ruth back hard, finally pulling away to give her a grateful smile.

'Thanks for taking me under your wing; I really needed the company today,' she said.

'You're welcome, sweetheart. We're flying back to England tomorrow so I'm afraid we won't be able to continue on your travels with you. I hope you enjoy your time in Capri, though—and that you find what you're looking for,' she said with a kind smile.

Indigo couldn't help but smile back, albeit with a twist of sad scepticism.

'Yeah, you never know,' she said.

And now here she was, stepping off the ferry in Capri into the bright morning sunshine and the first person she laid eyes on was Julien.

He appeared to have been watching the people getting off the ferry and as soon as he locked eyes with her he stood up and started walking towards her.

She came to a sudden halt in shock, feeling the other passengers push past her and hearing the odd 'tut' as she blocked part of the gangway. Her heart hammered in her chest, her senses on high alert as she watched him pushing his way through the crowd.

What was he doing here?

Pulling herself together, she started walking towards him again, feeling the tide of people drawing them ever closer together, until finally they were standing only feet apart, grinning as if they'd not seen each other for a year.

A gentle breeze whipped her hair around her head and she pushed it away from her face with a shaking hand.

'Julien—I thought I'd seen the last of you,' she said, hyperaware of a tremble in her voice. 'Were you waiting here for me?'

'*Oui.*'

She gazed into his eyes looking for a clue as to why, hardly daring to hope that he'd come to tell her he'd changed his mind about being ready for a new relationship, but his expression was inscrutable.

'I wanted to catch you before I leave Capri and sail on to Naples,' he said, taking her hand

and leading her gently away from the crowd of people still mingling around the ferry and over towards the quieter side of the port.

So he wasn't staying on Capri? Was he here to try and persuade her to leave with him then? The idea of it made her stomach flutter.

When they reached a small stone bench next to a closed ticket office he let go of her hand and, reaching for her rucksack, lifted it from her shoulder and propped it up against the bench.

The anticipation was killing her. 'What's going on? Is everything okay?' she asked, hugging her arms around her. Despite her conviction they were meant to be together, something in the back of her brain warned her not to get her hopes up, just in case.

'I have something I want to give you.' He moved his hand around to his back pocket, glancing behind him as he removed whatever he had in there.

For one ridiculous, heart-thumping second she

thought he was going to produce a ring and she drew in a sharp, shaky breath…

It was a large white envelope.

He held it out towards her, an expectant smile lighting up his eyes.

She tried hard not to let her disappointment show on her face as she stared down at it.

'What's this?' she asked.

'Open it and see.'

Her hands shook as she took the envelope from him and lifted up the flap at the back.

She stared at the contents, a heavy sinking sensation turning her stomach over.

It was money. Lots and lots of money. All in fifty euro notes.

'It's a donation to help with the running of your café. So you can keep working there,' he said, not appearing to notice her distress.

'I felt bad about the way we'd left things after what happened between us,' he said. 'I kept thinking about what a struggle you'll have when you get back to London. I wanted to do something to help you.'

'You came here to give me money?' she asked, her voice barely making it past her throat. Bitter disillusionment coursed through her, causing her eyes to burn with unshed tears and her skin to prickle as if she were being attacked by a thousand bees.

He frowned, looking visibly shocked by her lack of enthusiasm. 'What's wrong? I thought you'd be pleased.'

'Do you even know me at all? Did you really think I wouldn't be offended by you giving me money after I'd slept with you?' Her voice crackled with dismay. 'It's like you're paying me off to relieve your conscience!'

She knew it was a low blow, but she was so angry with him right now. Couldn't he see how humiliating this was for her?

'That's not why I'm giving it to you. *Mon Dieu!* It just means if your grant doesn't come through you can keep working there until you find another source of funding.' His shoulders tensed as he folded his arms across his chest. 'I wanted to do something to help you,' he repeated, in the same tone he'd used with the receptionist on the very first night they'd met, when he'd made it clear how disgusted he was with the lack of service she'd provided.

'I don't want your money, Julien.' This time the words came out loud and clear, thanks to a sudden surge of anger that came rushing up from the pit of her stomach.

He opened his mouth to speak, then looked away as if he'd thought better of it, frowning and shaking his head in confusion.

When he looked back, his expression was shuttered and a muscle flickered in his jaw.

'Where is this coming from, Indigo? Hmm? Why are you so angry with me for wanting to help? Can't you put your stubborn pride aside for a moment and let someone help *you* for once?' He shook his head, his eyes narrowed. 'I don't understand. What is it you want from me?'

How could he ask that? Didn't he know how she felt about him? Wasn't it obvious? 'I want you, you idiot!'

The silence after her outburst seemed to stretch on forever.

Finally, Julien closed his eyes and rubbed a hand over his face, letting out a long sigh.

'When you turned up here I thought you'd come back for me. *Me*, Julien!' Her throat felt painfully tight as she fought back the tears. 'But I guess that makes me the idiot!' A sob broke loose and she clasped a hand over her mouth to stop any more from escaping.

'Indigo—' His expression was full of regret now.

'I just want the opportunity for us to get to know each other better.' She took a deep, calming breath, not wanting to give in to her emotions and ruin any chance she had of making herself heard. 'To give a relationship a chance.'

He was shaking his head now, his eyes a little wild, as if she'd caught him in a trap and he couldn't see any way to escape. 'I can't, Indigo. I'm not ready for that.'

'So you'll just let this amazing connection that we have go? You feel it too, right? Please tell me it's not just me.'

There was another long silence where he stared at the ground. 'It's not just you,' he said finally.

'So why won't you give it a chance?'

'I *can't*, Indigo.'

'What are you afraid of?'

He rubbed a hand over his face. 'I've spent the last two years feeling like I was suffocating. I need my space—to begin to feel like I've got a grip on my life again.'

'And you can't do that and still have some space left for me?'

He spread his hands in mute apology. 'No. I'm sorry.' He gestured towards the envelope still clutched in her hand. 'That's the best I can do right now.'

'Well, I don't want it.' She thrust it back towards him and after a second's hesitation he took it from her.

From the intensity of his frown she could tell that he wasn't prepared to listen to any more of her entreaties.

She opened her mouth to try anyway, but he raised his hand to stop her.

'I can't ask you to wait for me, Indigo, because I don't know when I'll feel ready to have another serious relationship again—or if I'll ever be ready for one. And, after what happened with your ex, the last thing you need is to embark on something so precarious with someone like me. I don't want to have any part in corrupting that amazing positivity that you have. I'm too bitter and messed up right now. I'd be a danger to you.'

'But you might feel differently one day?' There was a pleading tone in her voice now that made her cringe inside.

'*Oui*, I might. But I can't make that promise and it wouldn't be fair to ask you to wait in the hope things would change for me. I need my freedom right now and you need something I can't give you—stability. Don't wait for me. I'm sure the best person for you will walk into your life when you most need him to.'

'You already did, Julien.' Her voice broke on his name.

He shook his head and backed away from her, the expression in his eyes hard with determination. '*Non*, Indigo. I think you're an amazing woman and at another time in my life maybe we could have had something really special, but not now.'

She moved towards him, desperate not to leave things this way between them. 'You can't beat yourself up forever because of one bad relationship.'

'I'm sorry, Indigo, I have nothing else to offer you right now.' He held up the envelope, then dropped his hand again as if he felt frustrated to still be holding it.

The pause seemed to go on forever as she

swallowed and swallowed and swallowed down the pain.

'Okay then, go, if that's what you think is best,' she finally managed to say.

He gave her one last nod, then turned and walked away, taking her very last hope for a future together with him.

She wanted to weep—for what could have been if only they'd met at another time.

How was it possible to feel like this for Julien after such a short amount of time? It seemed incredible that it was only a week since he'd come storming into her life with his reluctant heroism and inimitable strength.

But who you fell in love with wasn't something you could control.

And she had fallen in love with him. Desperately and completely.

But now she had to let him go.

There was something very fitting about the rough assault of waves against his boat, Julien reflected as he fought to keep the vessel on course through a sudden and ferocious storm that had swept in without warning the following day. It harmonised well with the raging confusion of emotions in his head.

This holiday was meant to punctuate a difficult and painful time in his life, to give him a definite end to the way it was then, but, to his utter frustration, it only seemed to have started a new chapter.

During his time with Indigo he'd begun to sense a difference in himself. Somehow she'd managed to pop the bubble that had been preventing him from feeling anything, bringing everything into razor-sharp focus.

The flip side of that was that he now felt everything. So acutely it made his chest ache.

He spent the next couple of days after the storm taking mental breaths whilst gliding slowly through the now peaceful waters, sailing past the looming greatness of Vesuvius, then onward towards his final destination, Naples, where he was to leave the boat and board a plane back to Paris.

Back to reality.

Not that this holiday hadn't been very real. In fact, it had probably ended up being more stressful than a week's work would have been, just for very different reasons.

Or, more precisely, one reason.

Not allowing himself to be with Indigo.

When he'd seen the look of appeal on her face, just before he'd turned away from her, he'd known in that split second what was causing the painful ache in his chest.

Love.

A fierce and irrepressible love for her.

It had shaken him to his core. Which was why he'd walked away and kept on walking until he was back on his boat, then back out to sea, putting a whole body of water between them.

He'd told himself at the time that he was leaving so she didn't get hurt, but he knew he'd only hurt her more. He'd seen it in her eyes and in the slump of her shoulders—the grief for something that could have been so good.

Thinking about it now, he realised he'd treated her with a total lack of respect by trying to buy his absolution.

How could he have thought that the way to make her happy was to give her *money*? How crass and unthinking he'd been. He knew now he couldn't buy her happiness or respect; he had to earn it with his actions, by giving her something of himself.

Which was a terrifying thought after what had happened with Celine. But then wasn't that the point? Real love was never easy; it was complex and sticky and downright rough sometimes.

He knew now that he hadn't been in love with Celine—in lust, sure—and he'd married her because he believed it was the right thing to do at the time. But the way he felt about Indigo wasn't wrapped up in sex or lust or duty; it was based on how he felt about himself when he was with her.

She'd made him come alive.

In the dark hours of the night, tossing and turning as sleep eluded him, he pictured her back in London, filling her days working at the café, laughing and joking with her colleagues, then perhaps going on a date with a man she'd met, the sparkle returning to her eyes as he lavished the praise and attention on her that she deserved.

The thought of someone else taking care of her made his stomach lurch with anxiety.

Indigo would be fine without him because she was a fighter. It was one of the things he loved about her.

But would he be all right without her?

Okay, so meeting Indigo right now wasn't great timing, but then what in life ever really was?

And at least this time being with her would be his choice.

Fuelled by the fervour of his revelation, he quickly plotted a course that would get him to Naples ahead of schedule, then picked up his phone, intent on getting himself out of Italy as fast as possible in order to set a new plan in motion.

He knew now that being here alone had been a pilgrimage to nothing. He'd thought he wanted his freedom—but it didn't feel the way he'd thought it would. It felt empty. And silent. And lonely.

A pyrrhic victory.

He'd thought he could go back to the way things used to be, before Celine, but trying to go backwards was a big mistake.

What he needed was a fresh start.

Finally, there was clarity in his mind. He missed Indigo. He loved her. He'd let her go.

And now he was going to get her back.

CHAPTER TEN

London is a vibrant and forward-looking city, ever evolving, with an exciting new encounter just waiting for you at every turn...

One week later

INDIGO WIPED HER hands on her apron and looked round at the eclectic gathering of local people who had turned up for her early evening cookery course, despite the torrential rain.

Her feet throbbed and her back ached from being on her feet all day, but her insides burned with satisfied warmth as she perused the table full of nutritious, delicious-smelling food that her class had produced in just half an hour—which they'd easily be able to replicate at home.

This made all her hard work worth it—the

shine of pride on the faces of people who'd previously not believed they'd ever have the skills
to cook anything vaguely edible for themselves,
let alone something they'd be proud to share with
friends or loved ones.

The kitchen at the back of the café wasn't
stocked with enough culinary equipment to be
able to teach more than five people at a time,
but she was hoping that once the grant came
through—she mentally crossed her fingers that
it still would—she'd be able to afford to buy
more so she could teach a larger group at one
time.

'Well, I think you've all done a wonderful job
today; it's great to see how much you've im-
proved since you first started coming here,' she
said, beaming at them all.

'It's good to have you back, Indigo; we missed
your lovely smile while you were off gallivant-
ing in Italy,' Ron, one of the gentlemen who
had been coming to her for a couple of months,
now called across the room, giving her a cheeky

wink. He'd been a morose character when he'd first started coming, due to losing his beloved wife only a short time ago, but he'd slowly made friends and come out of his shell as, week by week, he'd allowed himself to be integrated into the group. She suspected there might even be romance blossoming between him and the only lady currently attending. They often had their heads together, chatting quietly as they worked.

Pushing away a sting of melancholy at the thought of the dire state of her own love life, he returned his wink and gestured towards the table.

'Okay, well, if you want to start tidying away, we're just about out of time. I don't know about you, but I can't wait to get home and eat after being tortured by the smell of your wonderful grub cooking for the last twenty minutes.'

It was hard keeping up a chipper tone of voice when her heart was so heavy, but somehow she seemed to be managing it.

When the group had asked her about her holiday she'd worked hard to sound breezy and up-beat about it, telling them as much as she could whilst studiously avoiding mentioning Julien's name. She thought she'd pulled off making it sound as if she'd had a fun and revitalising time, though.

The bell of the café rang in the distance and she glanced over to her friend and kitchen assistant, Lacey, sharing a questioning smile with her.

'I'll go and see who it is and tell them we're closed,' Lacey said, already walking towards the door.

Grabbing some dirty bowls from the table, Indigo went to stack them in the dishwasher—wanting to pre-empt the tidy-up so she could get home a bit earlier tonight and have a soothing bath—and turned back to see Lacey walk into the kitchen, closely followed by a man.

A man who was tall, with blond hair and mesmerising whisky-brown eyes.

'Julien?' she gasped, not wanting to trust her

vision. She hadn't been sleeping particularly well since she'd got back, her mind still whirling with thoughts about him, and she wondered for a second whether her addled brain had conjured him up to torture her a little bit more.

He walked slowly towards her, smiling in that wry way that she knew so well, making her heart beat a little faster with the comforting familiarity of it.

'What…what are you doing here?' she stammered.

'I hear you offer cookery courses to men who no longer have wives,' he said.

She blinked at him, confused by such a strange opening line. 'To widowers usually,' she said uncertainly. There was a beat of uncomfortable silence. 'But I guess we could make an exception for a divorcee,' she finished, not wanting to look rude and uncomfortable in front of her class.

'Is this the young man you met on holiday that you've been avoiding telling us about?' Margery, the lone woman in the group, piped up, her eyes twinkling with good humour.

The whole roomful of people seemed to shift at once as they all turned to look at each other, exchanging knowing glances.

Had they been talking about her behind her back whenever she left the room?

She sighed, feeling trapped and unprepared to deal with Julien's presence here in her kitchen— a place she liked to think of as her personal sanctuary. 'This is Julien,' she said, gesturing vaguely towards him. 'And yes, we met in Italy.'

There was a murmur of friendly greeting from the group.

Turning to face him now, she said with as much assertiveness as she could muster, 'I'm afraid we're just about to pack up for the evening, but if you'd like to come back at another time I'm sure we can talk about finding a place in a group for you.'

There was a glint of determination in his eyes. 'Actually, I was hoping I could walk you home tonight,' he said, moving closer. 'I have some things I need to say to you—and I'd rather not do it in front of all these strange people.' He held up an apologetic hand to the group. 'No offence.'

'None taken,' Margery called from the other side of the room, giving Julien a supportive grin.

'Yes, Indigo, you go,' Lacey said. 'I can supervise the tidy-up and make sure the place is locked up before I leave.'

Indigo opened her mouth to argue but, as one, the whole group shook their heads at her.

'Go and spend some time with your friend,' Ron said, flapping a dismissing hand at her.

Well, it seemed as if she didn't have much of a choice. Clearly, they weren't going to let her stay. So much for her being the one in charge here.

'Okay then,' she said with an exasperated smile, pulling off her apron and going to hang it up on one of the pegs on the wall. She gave her hands a quick wash, then went to fetch her bag and coat from the small office behind the kitchen, taking a moment to drag in some steadying breaths before she went back out there to face whatever was in store for her this evening. No way was she letting herself get excited about him being here. She didn't think she could cope with more disappointment when it came to Julien.

When she returned he was chatting comfortably with Lacey, who was leaning against the counter, looking up at him with big, friendly eyes.

Huh, trust him to charm everyone as soon as he walked in.

'Okay, I'm ready to go,' she told Julien as she approached the two of them, making sure to keep her voice emotion-free. 'Thanks, Lacey.'

'Have a good evening,' her friend replied, giving her a covert eyebrow-waggle.

Indigo scowled back, intensely aware of Julien's presence right there beside her.

'See you next week, everyone,' she called to the rest of the group, hoping to goodness her face didn't look as flushed as it felt. They all responded with a wave and a smile and continued to watch her with interest until she put her hand on Julien's back and ushered him towards the door. There was a gentle hubbub of noise as they walked out. No doubt tongues would be wagging once she'd gone.

Out in the damp night air, she turned to face him and crossed her arms in front of her. It felt so strange to see him here, on her patch. He was as immaculately dressed as always and her tummy tumbled as she fully took him in for the first time since he'd shown up. He looked so darn handsome, standing there as if he didn't have a care in the world. Which she guessed he didn't. She wondered fleetingly whether it was going to be possible to get through this without entirely losing her cool.

'So what's this all about? Why are you here?'

He let out a low breath and looked around him, as if gathering himself for what he was about to say. 'Let's walk, shall we?'

'Can't you just tell me here?' she said, grasping on to the only thread of power she had left.

He crossed his own arms and frowned down at the floor and she noticed for the first time that he had a black shopping bag swinging from one hand. She wondered what he could have in there. It was a strange receptacle for him to be carrying overnight clothes in.

'What's in the bag?' she blurted, unable to keep her curiosity to herself.

'You'll see,' he said, flashing her an enigmatic smile.

'Really? You're not going to tell me?'

'*Non*. You'll have to wait until we're back at your flat and I'm ready to show you. I'm not prepared to do this out on the street either.'

She bristled with frustration. 'And you think I'm stubborn!' Sighing, she took one more look at the determination on his face and gave him a resigned nod, knowing there was no way she could turn him away. Not if it meant she'd finally find out what was really going on with him. It had been eating away at her since she'd last seen him and she needed answers so she could move on.

'Okay, fine, you win.' She gestured for them to start walking. 'It's this way.'

It only took them two minutes to walk to her flat from the café and neither of them spoke a word as they made their way down the noisy main road, stepping around the puddles that the earlier heavy downpour had left in its wake.

'This is me,' she said when they reached the end of her road.

He followed her to her flat—the place she'd moved into after Gavin had left her. Hers was on the top floor of the converted terrace house, which she loved because she enjoyed falling asleep looking at the night sky through the sky-light in the sloping attic ceiling.

'I'm at the top,' she said, letting them in through the main door and leading him up the stairs. It took her a moment to get the key to line up with the lock because her hands were shaking so much. He stood so close to her she could smell the wonderfully evocative scent of him and she had to take great gulps of air through her mouth so as not to become too distracted by the urge to turn around and wrap her arms around him and pull him close.

When she finally got the door open, she led him through to the kitchen diner and gestured for him to sit with her at the small dining table that she had set up in the middle of the room.

Blood pulsed in her ears as she waited for him to tell her why he was here.

'Have you heard about your grant yet?' he asked conversationally, throwing her for a loop.

Was he still cross about her refusing to take the money from him? She hoped he wasn't here to try and get her to change her mind. She didn't regret the decision she'd made, firmly believing that things would work out here without his help. Somehow.

She folded her arms. 'Not yet. Soon, hopefully.'

'That must be stressful.'

She shrugged. 'Yes, well, as you know, money and I aren't exactly on speaking terms at the moment.'

He smiled. 'That makes two of us.'

What did he mean by that?

'Are you having financial troubles too?' she asked, confused.

'No. But money seems to be my nemesis at the moment. It makes me do stupid things.'

There was a tense pause while she waited for him to elaborate.

He didn't. Instead, he jumped up and started pacing around the room, moving into the living area and running his fingers lightly over her things, as if wanting to learn them by touch.

'It's a great flat. Exactly the sort of place I imagined you living in. It's very you.'

'Me?'

He nodded, turning to look her in the eyes. 'Sophisticated, but welcoming.'

She couldn't stop the smile from breaking over her face. 'How very kind of you.'

He started pacing around again and she realised with a shock that he was nervous.

Standing up, she took a couple of steps towards him. 'Julien, will you please just spit out whatever it is you've come to say? You're killing me here!'

He stopped moving and turned to face her again, his expression apologetic.

Taking an audible breath, he walked closer. 'Okay, first of all, I wanted to say sorry, about trying to buy my freedom—and your forgiveness. It was a crass and selfish thing to do. I knew how much you needed that money and it wasn't fair to make you choose between that and me.' He snorted gently. 'Not that you did. In your inimitable style you turned your back on both options.'

'I couldn't feel like I was indebted to you, Julien, it would have destroyed any equilibrium between us.'

He nodded, his expression telling her he understood what she was saying. 'It seems to have become a bad habit with me to throw money at things to try and fix them quickly and without pain. It was ignorant of me to do that and I can see now why you were offended. I apologise.'

A heavy weight seemed to lift from her chest. 'Apology accepted.'

Julien looked at the woman he loved and knew that if he wanted to repair things between them he had to tell her everything. He owed her an explanation after all the strife he'd caused. But now he was here he was having trouble finding the words he needed without making himself sound like the worst kind of low life.

This was exactly why he'd not talked to anyone else when it became apparent that his marriage was over. The shame had stopped the words—kept them lodged inside him, somewhere between his chest and his throat, like a cork pushed too far down to extract.

'I want to tell you why I was such a nightmare to be around in Italy,' he said. 'So you understand that my behaviour was never about something you did or didn't do.'

The apprehension in her eyes made his blood pump faster and he watched with concern as she walked further into the living area and sat down heavily on to her small red velvet sofa as if her legs had suddenly refused to hold her any longer.

'Okay. Go on,' she said quietly.

He sat down too and turned to face her, making sure he had her full attention before he started his sorry tale.

She looked back at him with such apprehension he hoped to God this wouldn't be the last time he'd ever see her after making his confession.

'My ex-wife's name is Celine,' he began, deciding to cover the basic facts first, hoping the rest would flow from there. 'We met at a mutual friend's wedding. Both of us were late and we snuck into the back of the church together and somehow managed to knock over a huge flower display and disrupt the service at a key moment. As you can imagine, that didn't exactly make us popular guests, but it banded us together as social fugitives.'

'Is your mutual friend speaking to you yet?' she asked with a smile in her voice.

He grimaced, too aware of the regret pulling at him to enjoy the gentle joke, but relieved that she felt comfortable enough to tease him still. 'Only just.'

She flapped a hand. 'Sorry to interrupt; do go on.'

'At that point in my life I'd been working so hard I'd not given any of my relationships—with perfectly nice women—a decent chance of surviving and it had begun to occur to me, as I watched all my friends get married and move on with their lives, that I'd put my career before my personal life for too long, and if I didn't do something about it I was going to end up a lonely old man.'

She shifted on the sofa, pulling her legs under her, and he took her cue and settled back, making himself more comfortable.

'Celine made me feel like there could be an exciting future ahead of me and, after our first meeting, we started seeing each other regularly—though when I say "seeing" I mean we spent a lot of time in bed together. It was a crazy whirlwind of a relationship and she turned my entire world upside down. She had this energy that electrified me: she was wild and spontaneous and creative, all the things I'm not, but she was also highly strung and only seemed to thrive when all the attention was on her. I can see that now, with the benefit of hindsight, though I was blind to it at the time.'

He was quiet for a while as he relived the memory of what he'd thought was the most passionate and extraordinary interlude in his formerly routine life—until he'd met Indigo and realised what passion really was.

'So what happened?' she prompted gently.

He sighed. 'We jumped into getting married too quickly.' He took a breath. 'I thought I was doing the right thing at the time, but it was a huge mistake.'

'What do you mean, "doing the right thing"?' she asked with a careful tone to her voice, which made him think she'd already figured it out.

He turned to give her a sad, knowing smile. '*Oui*, she was pregnant.'

She looked at him steadily for a moment and he saw her throat bob as she swallowed hard. 'Ah. I see. Well, that was honourable of you.'

'Yes, well, my father left my mother after he got her pregnant and she struggled for money and support for years, raising me. It was very tough on her. I didn't want Celine to suffer like that and I wanted to be there for my child. I worked hard for years to be successful so I'd be in a good position to support a family, should I have one. It didn't happen the way I was expecting it to, but I thought: *so what?* This was my child and I was prepared to make a go of the marriage so we could all be together.'

'So you *do* have a child?' she asked quietly.

He shook his head and averted his gaze, staring instead at a print of Monet's *Poppies* that she had on the wall behind the sofa, finding comfort in the vibrant colours. '*Non*. We lost the baby a few weeks after our wedding.'

When he turned back to look at her, the expression on her face was so full of sympathy it made his stomach drop.

'Oh, Julien, I'm so sorry to hear that.'

He nodded to acknowledge her commiseration. 'It wasn't just the failed pregnancy that wrecked our relationship, though,' he continued. 'It felt to me as though Celine gave up her individuality as soon as we got married, as if she didn't need to try at anything any more. She'd already handed in her notice at the place she worked and I became her whole universe. It was stifling. She wanted my undivided attention and I tried to give her as much as I could, but she'd phone me ten or twenty times a day and turn up when I had important meetings and make a scene if I didn't have time to see her.'

'Was this before or after the miscarriage?' Indigo asked.

'Before. It got even worse after it.'

Indigo didn't say anything, just nodded as if she understood.

'Then, when we lost the baby, she didn't want me to even leave the house. She became obsessed with trying to get pregnant again, to the point where there was no joy in our sex life any more. It was as if she only thought of me as a baby-making machine and would get angry with me if I said I was too tired or not in the mood. When I suggested we should wait a while before trying to get pregnant again, to give us both some time to recover, she was furious with me. So furious.'

He rubbed a hand over his face, feeling the familiar tension mounting.

'I tried to get her friends to talk to her, to give

her the kind of support I couldn't,' he said, wanting Indigo to know he hadn't been totally heartless about it, 'but she froze them out, saying they couldn't possibly understand how she felt. She hadn't spoken to her parents in years—she and her father had had some kind of falling out when she was eighteen—so there was no support there either. And she refused to go to counselling. She wanted me to make things better, but I had no idea how to make her happy any more. It got too much. I started working later and later and ignoring her calls, just to get some space.'

The words seemed to be pouring from him now, as if the pressure they'd been stoppered under had finally found a release.

'Then she stopped talking to me, to punish me, I think, and my life outside work became one long, silent nightmare. So then I spent even more time away from the house so I didn't have to face what had gone wrong with my life.'

'Oh, Julien, that sounds horrendous.' She put

her hand briefly over his and he found comfort in the warmth of her touch. But only for a moment.

'It wasn't the best year of my life, that's for sure.'

'So who ended it?'

'She did. She told me she wanted a divorce out of the blue one morning, then walked out and didn't come back.'

'That must have been difficult for you.'

'Honestly—I didn't try very hard to stop her.' He sighed and scrubbed a hand through his hair, making it stand on end. 'I didn't love her.'

'Oh, Julien—'

But he didn't want her sympathy right then, didn't feel as if he deserved it. 'She needed more from me. She needed my understanding. I knew she wasn't coping well with the miscarriage, but I kept pushing her away because I didn't know how to deal with everything that had happened either. I failed her.'

He felt Indigo move closer to him on the sofa. 'You mustn't think that. It must have been awful for both of you and it sounds like she fell apart and expected you to deal with everything. You shouldn't feel guilty for not trying harder. It sounds like you did everything you could think of.'

'I offered her a very generous divorce settlement to get it over with quickly. At least she'll never need to work another day in her life. I fixed her with money.' He let out a long, low rush of breath. 'And I feel relieved to be free of her. That makes me a terrible person, doesn't it?'

He glanced over at Indigo and was relieved to see understanding in her eyes.

On his way here he'd been terrified about how she'd take all this. He'd almost turned back a couple of times, but he knew if he wanted her he had to have the courage to tell her everything.

'It doesn't make you a terrible person. It makes you human,' she said, giving his hand a squeeze this time. 'And it doesn't sound like there was much of a relationship to save after you lost the baby.'

He picked up her hand from where it lay in her lap and linked his fingers through hers, feeling her shiver at his touch. The discovery that she felt the same way he did gave him courage.

'*Oui*. It became clear pretty quickly that we didn't have a lot in common after we got married. We thought and reacted to things in completely contrary ways. When we found out she was pregnant I told myself it wouldn't matter that we were so different because we'd have the child to hold us together.'

'It sounds like there was a good chance the marriage wouldn't have worked even if the baby had survived, and then you'd have felt guilty about depriving him or her of a stable family background instead.'

'Perhaps,' he said, letting her words wash though his mind. It felt good to have finally said all this out loud, after it had festered in his head for so long.

'Have you talked to someone? A counsellor or a friend?'

'*Non.*'

'Why not?'

'Because I'm fine.'

'But you lost a child too.'

'I'm *fine.*'

'So I get it now,' Indigo said, screwing up her face in sympathy.

He gave her a puzzled look. 'Get what?'

'The enforced solitude in Italy. You were making yourself walk the coast path alone as a penance—because you were punishing yourself for not doing more to save your marriage.'

'I didn't do a very good job of being on my own, though,' he said, forcing irony into his smile.

'Perhaps that's because, deep down, you know there was nothing you could have done to make things better, but you feel like you should punish yourself anyway.'

'Or I just couldn't keep away from you, no matter how hard I tried.'

'I'm glad you didn't,' she whispered, looking

deep into his eyes, and he knew for sure. at that moment, it hadn't been a mistake to come here. She loved him as fiercely as he loved her. He could see it there, written plainly on her face.

And now he wanted to show her how much she meant to him.

'Are you hungry?' he asked. 'You must be after working with food all day.'

'A bit,' she said, giving him a baffled smile.

'Good, because I managed to get hold of the recipe for that pasta dish you liked so much in the beach restaurant in Nerano. I have all the ingredients in there.' He pointed to the black shopping bag he'd left on the kitchen counter.

She stared at him, clearly shocked at this revelation. 'You persuaded them to tell you their secret?'

'*Oui.*'

'And you're going to cook it for me?'

'Sure I am.'

She raised an eyebrow at him, the expression

in her eyes wary. Clearly, she still wasn't entirely sure what he'd come here for.

'Are you trying to woo me with your culinary skills?' she asked hesitantly, confirming his suspicions.

'You might want to taste my food before you decide whether it's woo-worthy. I'm not as experienced as you. To be honest, I very rarely cook.' He flashed her a smile. 'But I like a challenge.'

'I'm sure it'll be delicious,' she said, her eyes wide with badly concealed bewilderment, 'but I'm happy to lend a hand.' She started to get up from the sofa.

'Non.' He held up a finger, gesturing for her to stay where she was. 'You sit down and relax. I'll fetch you a glass of wine and you can watch me work.'

Indigo watched in baffled pleasure as Julien made a production of opening an expensive-looking bottle of wine, searching through her cupboards till he'd found her paltry selection of glasses, pouring a large measure into one of them and handing it to her, then going back to the counter to unpack the bag he'd brought with him.

There was something wonderful about watching him moving around her kitchen, preparing and cooking a meal especially for her. Being the one who was looked after for once.

'I'm moving to London, Indigo,' he said suddenly as he dropped pasta into a pan of bubbling water. 'I've decided to branch out and set up a new arm to the business that focuses on providing affordable housing for first-time buyers and low-wage families.'

She stared at him. 'Wow, that sounds amazing.'

He was moving? Here, to London? Her heart tripped over itself at the news.

He looked up at her, flashing her a smile. 'You inspired me.'

'Me?'

'Yes, you. After you told me about your community café it made me realise that I've been too profit-focused for too long. I want to make a difference in people's lives too. And that's the best way I can employ my existing skills and knowledge in order to do that.'

'Well, I think that's wonderful, Julien, but I thought you loved living in Paris?'

'I do, but you're not there.'

The shock of his words reverberated through her head, making her feel a little dizzy.

'You'd move here for me?'

'*Oui*. If we're to give a relationship a chance we need to be living in the same city, since we're both very busy people.'

She gaped at him, her mind reeling as a small but persistent bubble of hope pushed upwards.

'Anyway, you persuaded me whilst we were away that London could come a close second to Paris,' he continued, abandoning what he was doing at the counter and walking back over to her at the sofa. 'And it won't take long to travel back there for a weekend when I need a fix. I can introduce you to my favourite parts of the city. I'd like that.'

He sat down next to her, taking her hands.

'But what if it didn't work out between us?' she asked warily, unable to ignore the memory of how badly things had gone with Gavin. She didn't want to feel responsible for Julien giving up everything he loved if it made him miserable.

'Someone once told me that you've just got to keep positive and everything will work itself out in the end.'

'Someone once told me that was total claptrap,' she pointed out.

'That guy was an idiot.'

She closed her eyes and smiled. When she opened them again he was looking at her with an expression of utter seriousness.

'I've had enough time on my own to think about things. When we talked in Capri I was afraid—afraid that I couldn't give you the level of attention you deserve, that I couldn't be positive enough for you, that you'd come to resent me for my dour outlook and selfish moods. I didn't want you to think of me like that. I wanted to be ready and capable of showing you the real me. Not the shell of a man I was when we first met. It nearly killed me, walking away, but I had to be sure I could handle it.'

'And are you?'

'*Oui*. After panicking that I might have lost you, and realising that would make me so much more miserable, I *know* I can now.'

Indigo swallowed hard, feeling a familiar tightness in her throat, only this time it was from overwhelming excitement.

He leaned forwards, stroking his thumbs over the backs of her hands. 'I've thought about you every single day since I left you, Indigo. Pretty much every minute of every day. What we had felt so right—no matter how much I tried to convince myself it wasn't—and in a way that it never did with Celine, or anyone else I've ever met. As soon as I met you I *knew*.'

'Me too,' she whispered.

He smiled, relief lighting up his eyes. 'I want to be near you so we can make a real go of a relationship. If you want that too. What do you say? Has fate kept my slot open for me?'

She was so excited by what he was saying, but she still couldn't stop a deep-seated worry from tugging at her.

'What is it?' he asked, clearly sensing her in-decision.

'I'm worried that I get too argumentative around you and that you'll get fed up with it.'

'You mean your fighting spirit? I love that you stand up for yourself.'

She felt a smile pull at the corners of her mouth.

'But what if I become really self-centred again? I need to be able to concentrate on the café to keep it running and I might not always be around when you need me.'

'You mean you'd put yourself first for once? Instead, of always considering other people's feelings before your own? I think I could handle that.' He flashed her a wry grin. 'I want to be here to support you, Indigo. Not with money,' he added quickly when he saw the look on her face, 'but to be here when you need me. In fact, I'd live in a cardboard box if it meant I could be with you. The money, the possessions, they mean nothing to me; they're just noise. I have far more than I need to be happy and if me having money makes you uncomfortable then you can help me decide where it could best be donated in order to help other people.'

She stared at him. 'You'd be willing to do that?'

'Yes. For the woman I love.'

'Love—?' She could barely say the word as her throat filled with happy tears.

'Oui.' He nodded. 'I'm in love with you.'

'Oh, thank goodness,' she said in a rush, 'because I'm in love with you too.'

There was a look of acute happiness in his eyes as he lifted his hand and slid it into her hair, angling her head towards him and crushing his lips against hers, kissing her with such passion it took her breath away.

When he eventually pulled back she almost growled with frustration, until he cupped his palms around her jaw and looked deep into her eyes.

'Yes, I'm in love with you, Indigo. I love you for your strength and your determination. Your generosity when you have nothing left to give. Your kindness to a strange Frenchman who needed someone to take an interest in him and make him feel like he had something left to offer. That's why I love you. Because you remind me of all the good things about me that I'd forgotten about. You're the person I'm supposed to have my happy-ever-after with. I believe that now.'

'I believe it too.'

'Good.'

He kissed her again, even more thoroughly this time.

'I want it all with you, Indigo,' he said, kissing her nose, her eyes. 'A home, a family…' He kissed her forehead, her cheeks. 'A future.' Her drew back and smiled, deep into her eyes. 'But mostly I want you.'

She experienced a surge of pure joy at his words, knowing for certain now that this was meant to be. That this was fate and she could give him everything he wanted.

And more.

Much, much more.

EPILOGUE

When pondering what to do for your next adventure, you might want to consider something that has it all: excitement, good society and a plethora of opportunities for personal discovery...

Two years later

INDIGO PACED BACK and forth, quickly covering the floor space of the home that she and Julien had bought together after he'd whisked her off to Paris to propose, just six months after moving to London.

They'd fallen in love with the bijou but funky flat situated in a warehouse conversion in Brixton as soon as they'd walked into it. Since moving in, they'd had great fun decorating it simply but stylishly, haunting the antique and flea markets in both London and Paris until they'd managed to put together a collection of furniture that suited and reflected both of their tastes.

With the two of them sharing the mortgage, Indigo had been confident she could comfortably afford her half of the repayment with her wage from the Welcome Café, and she loved walking through the door and knowing that this place was just as much hers as it was Julien's.

It seemed like a long time ago now that she'd been worried about having to give up working at the café, but she still felt grateful every day for the grants that had turned up just in the nick of time, allowing them to expand and, more recently, open up new branches in other parts of the city. Even though she'd known Julien would have stepped in and given her as much money as she needed had the grants not appeared, she would never have taken it from him, needing to maintain her financial independence for her own sense of pride.

As it turned out, he'd needed to invest a lot of it in his not-for-profit affordable housing scheme, which had already brought happiness and security to a large number of people who had previously believed they'd never be able to afford their own home.

She was so proud of him for what he'd achieved in such a short space of time. He'd worked tirelessly to make it all happen and was full of positivity for expansion in the future.

It made her heart swell to see him so fired up and happy.

Even though they both led very independent working lives, they'd made sure they were around for each other whenever support was required—either as a sounding board to bounce ideas off, or just to be there to listen to each other talk about the vexations or achievements of their day.

Since they were both incredibly busy during the week, they made sure to take regular breaks away from the city at weekends, when they'd walk and camp and explore the most beautiful parts of England, and occasionally other European countries.

It was a solid and equal partnership, with both of them working hard to make sure they communicated any worries or frustrations they had well before they became an issue.

It worked.

But then she always knew it would. Because they both wanted it to.

Indigo could barely believe it had only been two years since they'd first met in Italy. It felt now as though she'd known him forever.

Their wedding, a year ago, had been a joyous affair, with family and friends travelling from far and wide to the beautiful rural estate just outside Paris—which had been loaned to them by a friend of Julien's—to celebrate with them.

Indigo had worried about how hard she might find it, not having either of her parents there to see her get married, and she'd shed a tear for their absence the night before, but she hadn't allowed it to taint her happiness during the day. She knew they were there with her, in her heart.

And she'd had plenty of people who loved her there, rooting for her. All of her brothers had come along with their families in tow, which had made for an entertaining and raucous gathering.

She and Julien had loved every second of it.

Walking into the kitchen, she gave the food in the oven one last check to make sure it would be ready to serve as soon as Julien walked through the door. She'd been planning this special meal since this morning, wanting to mark the occasion with style.

Even though Julien had insisted on her teaching him how to cook so they could share the task and give her a break from it when she'd been on her feet all day, she still loved to make food for him, just to see the look of delight on his face when she presented him with one of his favourite meals. He was the perfect recipient, making sure to let her know just how much he appreciated her efforts, showering her with affection and love afterwards.

She couldn't have asked for more.

Except for one thing.

She twisted the much treasured wedding and engagement rings round and round on her finger as she waited impatiently for Julien to get back from work and walk through the door.

Since the wedding they'd tried and failed to conceive, each month bringing with it a sense of crushed excitement as the possibility of extending their family failed to come to fruition.

They'd stayed upbeat about it, but she could tell just how much Julien longed for it to happen. She knew exactly how he felt because she wanted it just as fiercely.

Her heart bumped hard against her chest as she finally heard the sound of Julien's key in the front door, and she rushed to meet him, her blood racing with excitement to finally have him home.

He'd barely made it through the door when

she launched herself at him, throwing her arms around his neck and hugging him tightly to her.

'Whoa!' he said, nearly losing his balance, only managing to keep them both upright by grabbing hold of the doorjamb. 'That's quite a welcome. What's this about?'

Pulling away from him, and without saying a word, she reached into the back pocket of her jeans and brought out the little bit of magic she'd been checking and rechecking over and over again all day with a ceremonial flourish.

'Ta-da!'

He stared at it, perplexed, until the penny finally dropped. 'What does it say?' he asked, his voice shaking with anticipation.

She held it closer so he could read the words on the little screen.

'You're pregnant?' he said, his voice lifting with excitement.

'Yes!'

'How long have you known?'

'I did the test this morning.' She could barely talk for excitement.

'Why didn't you call me?' he said, grabbing her around the waist and lifting her up so he could swing her round and round.

'I knew you needed to be able to concentrate on the meeting with your investors today,' she said, laughing with elation at his reaction. 'I was worried you might go to pieces and they'd think you were a bit loopy and refuse to give you the money.'

He laughed and put her down, holding on to her until he was sure she had her balance, then flapping his hand in that Gallic way she loved so much. 'Go to pieces! Me! Never!' But there was a glint of tears in his eyes now.

Sliding her hands up to cup his jaw, she gently pulled him towards her so she could kiss his eyes, his nose, his mouth.

'You're a big softie really,' she murmured, kissing away a lone tear that had escaped from his eye.

'I'm just happy. I've wanted this so much.'

'Me too.'

He stroked her cheek, looking deep into her eyes.

'I'm so glad my child will have a mother like you.' He kissed her, his touch firm and possessive. 'Someone who is dedicated to bringing happiness to everyone she meets.' He kissed her again, the urgency of it reminding her how loved she was, how wanted. 'Someone who is full of love for others, no matter their situation.' This time the kiss went on and on until she was breathless with joy.

She couldn't believe how lucky she was to have him.

With each other's support and love they'd finally been able to close the book on the regrets of their pasts.

And now an exciting new chapter of their lives was about to begin.

* * * *

MILLS & BOON®
Large Print – September 2016

Morelli's Mistress
Anne Mather

A Tycoon to Be Reckoned With
Julia James

Billionaire Without a Past
Carol Marinelli

The Shock Cassano Baby
Andie Brock

The Most Scandalous Ravensdale
Melanie Milburne

The Sheikh's Last Mistress
Rachael Thomas

Claiming the Royal Innocent
Jennifer Hayward

The Billionaire Who Saw Her Beauty
Rebecca Winters

In the Boss's Castle
Jessica Gilmore

One Week with the French Tycoon
Christy McKellen

Rafael's Contract Bride
Nina Milne

MILLS & BOON®
Large Print – October 2016

Wallflower, Widow...Wife!
Ann Lethbridge

Bought for the Greek's Revenge
Lynne Graham

An Heir to Make a Marriage
Abby Green

The Greek's Nine-Month Redemption
Maisey Yates

Expecting a Royal Scandal
Caitlin Crews

Return of the Untamed Billionaire
Carol Marinelli

Signed Over to Santino
Maya Blake

Wedded, Bedded, Betrayed
Michelle Smart

The Greek's Nine-Month Surprise
Jennifer Faye

A Baby to Save Their Marriage
Scarlet Wilson

Stranded with Her Rescuer
Nikki Logan

Expecting the Fellani Heir
Lucy Gordon

MILLS & BOON®

Why shop at millsandboon.co.uk?

Each year, thousands of romance readers find their perfect read at millsandboon.co.uk. That's because we're passionate about bringing you the very best romantic fiction. Here are some of the advantages of shopping at www.millsandboon.co.uk:

* **Get new books first**—you'll be able to buy your favourite books one month before they hit the shops

* **Get exclusive discounts**—you'll also be able to buy our specially created monthly collections, with up to 50% off the RRP

* **Find your favourite authors**—latest news, interviews and new releases for all your favourite authors and series on our website, plus ideas for what to try next

* **Join in**—once you've bought your favourite books, don't forget to register with us to rate, review and join in the discussions

Visit **www.millsandboon.co.uk**
for all this and more today!